Hank

The First Novel
in
The Gunpowder Trilogy

Arch Montgomery

bancroft
press

Baltimore, MD

Published by Bancroft Press ("Books that enlighten")
P.O. Box 65360, Baltimore, MD 21209
800-637-7377
410-764-1967 (fax)
www.bancroftpress.com

Cover and interior design by Tammy Grimes, www.tsgcrescent.com, 814.941.7447
Cover illustration by Phyllis Montgomery

ISBN 1-890862-22-3
Library of Congress Control Number: 2002109256
Printed in the United States of America

First Edition

1 3 5 7 9 10 8 6 4 2

To Phyllis, Gregory, and Tyler

Chapter 1

My little league baseball coach is clueless. After every practice, he makes us run around the bases for minutes and minutes.

It's pointless. Anybody who knows anything about baseball knows that nobody runs, not even the best professional players. Like when was the last time anybody told Mark McGwire, "Get the lead out"? "OK, there, Mo Vaughan, if you don't run those bases, we're putting you right on your fat butt."

Yeah, right. Name me a pro manager who'd keep his job after saying something that stupid. The players make millions and never run. We're supposed to be having fun, but we're paying Coach to make us run around the bases? I'd thought he was a pretty sensible and smart guy. Right! He's crazy AND clueless.

Sue says she's known guys like Coach. She says people like him are control freaks who get off on bossing other people around. She says that it's my call whether to stay on the team or quit, seeing as I'm going into eighth grade and all. Sue, by the way, is my mom. I can call her Sue cause her new husband's "Pete," and we're on a first name basis. Sue says she doesn't have any "authority hang-ups." Coach sure does.

Plus he's not much for evaluating talent. I'm hitting over .500. I'm the best pitcher on the team. I got this wicked forkball that falls right off the table — that's got guys swinging at balls that bounce way in front of the plate. When I'm not on the mound, I play short. Together with my step-brother, Jake, who plays second and can turn the pivot better than any kid I ever seen, we've been turnin' double plays like crazy all season. Yup, Coach is gonna miss me big-time. He'll miss me all the rest of the season. 'Cause I quit. That's it. Screw the Coach and screw the whole effen team!

Besides, quitting the team'll give me more time for riding my bike this summer. I like bikin' the Gunpowder Falls Trail—lots of cool jumps there and, when it gets too hot, you can just ease off your bike and into the water. You should see all the tubers floating down the river on a real hot July day. They come in these big groups, screamin' and laughin,' all hooked together with their feet. I especially like the college girls who go tubin'. I like to look at them a lot. They sure know how to put on a bathing suit.

Anyway, college dudes always have coolers full of beer jammed into one tube and then coolers full of great sandwiches stuffed into another tube. I can usually weasel a brewski or a sandwich off of 'em. Pete calls beers brewskis, and he says it's better for me to learn how to drink the right way with him instead of going out and getting hammered by myself or with my crazy friends. Doing all that sounds pretty damn good to me.

Almost as much fun as the tubers are the fly fishermen at the Gunpowder River. God, those guys are major league serious. They've got their fancy rubber pants on and their flashy green or blue or red shirts — you know, the ones with all kinds of little pockets and zippers and who knows what other kind of stuff hanging off 'em. And then they've got their hats with "Tarponwear" on 'em, and there's gotta be some kind of rule that you need to wear lots of signs. This one guy had at least a dozen — I counted. There was "Orvis," and "LL Bean," and

"Eddie Bauer." I also saw "Sage" and "Leonard" and "Cabellos" and "On the Fly." There was more — I just can't remember 'em all.

I like watchin' those guys fish, too. They swish their fishing poles back and forth until their line gets tangled up in some tree. Then they slosh over to where they got all tangled up, and they curse. Then they break their line and curse some more. They'll stand real, real still after rummaging through their shirt pockets. Then they'll stare at their fingers and the end of the line like they're hypnotized or something, saying something like, "That ought to do it," under their breath. And you know what? Some of them'll turn right around and repeat the whole routine. But generally there's more cursing the second time around. They're so lame!

One guy made me laugh so hard I thought I was gonna puke, but he hears me and gets all red-faced and bent out of shape. "What are you laughing at, you little asshole?" he asks me. That makes me tip off my bike and start rolling on the ground. I swear I can't even breathe. Then he decides to try to catch me. No chance of that! I dust him. Does that guy really believe he isn't funny?

One Saturday morning in June, Jake and me go to our neighbor's pond and pull out this big old honker of a carp. He must weigh a coupla tons. He's lost all his color and is just kind of a sickly "I-ain't-never-seen-the-light-of-day" white. I clonk him on the head with my bicycle pump and shove him into Jake's backpack. Then we cycle up to what they call the catch and release area just below Pretty Boy Dam and a few 100 yards below Beaver Dam — you know, just before you get to Little Falls Road. So we dive down into one of the deeper pools, where some guys were having luck the day before. I'd say it's about five foot deep there. Well, it takes us the better part of an hour to get that old carp lookin' just the way we want, but we do it using some weights and some fishing line and a couple of half penny nails. There that honker of a carp sits, wavin' in the current.

For the rest of the week, after baseball practice, we sit up in the trees, watching our favorite fish and how the fishermen react when they get a load of him. I like the enthusiastic clueless guys the best. "Holy shit, Jack," says one. "Look at that trout." And then they just fish the hell out of that pool, real excited, feeling around in their pockets for new stuff to wave in front of a fish corpse. Honest to God, two guys kept up that lame routine for a whole hour.

Two other guys look down at the fish from a boulder at the foot of the pool. "Will you look at that," says the one with a mustache who's sucking on a pipe. "I can't believe the poor old Gunpowder has carp in it this high up. It must be all those damn bait fishermen ruining the river." I almost yell down from the tree, "No shit, Sherlock, but it's a dead carp, and you're a live idiot." But I don't.

My very favorite fisherman is this little sawed-off blond guy with no hat and a little Asian baby girl peeking out of a backpack just behind his neck. She has her own little fishing rod with a little cloth fish tied onto the end of the line, and she's waving it around and using it to whack the sawed-off guy on the head. The guy and the baby laugh and talk as they walk up to the pool, where two other guys are getting ready to go corpse fishing. The sawed-off guy stops and looks into the pool. He pauses just a second and looks back and forth between the two corpse fishers and asks, "What're you seeing down there?"

"Big trout," one guy says, pointing it out.

"It might be a carp," the sawed-off guy says after receiving another whack on the head from the baby.

"You think so?" the other guy says.

"Yup. Might even be a dead carp." With that said, the sawed-off dude and his baby girl head upstream with their rods, laughing and talking just like they were before. I like them a lot.

Stuff like that is about the only thing keeping this long summer from being a total waste for me. I admit I'm in a pissy mood. I want to go down to the shore with Sue and Pete, but they won't take any real vacations. Sue says that she and Pete may go down alone a few times, and she gives me this big wink and says, "We need time alone, honey. You know, I've got to keep my man."

I don't like it much when she talks that way. So I'll spend the weekends at Dad's. After church on Sunday, he lies on the couch all day reading the *New York Times*. Monday through Saturday, he busts his butt at work bein' a lawyer. I'd like to know him a little better, but I sure can't accuse him of being lazy or nothin'. Maybe he'd have gotten a kick out of seeing me throw my forkball in Little League earlier this summer, but he never could break from work long enough to get to a single game! Great supporter he is!

Being at Dad's house, which is mostly on weekends, really means being under the thumb of Mrs.-Perfect-Lady-Karen. Most of the time, that's a total disaster, except she has these two great kids of her own — my stepsister, Stephie, and my stepbrother and double-play partner, Jake. They keep me sane around the great lady. Little Stephie is pretty, funny, and easy to take. Jake is Jake.

Everything is on a schedule at Mrs.-Perfect-Lady's house — breakfast at eight, lunch at noon, dinner at seven. You miss a meal, she says, and there's no food for you, unless you call ahead. And she means it. At meals, you wear a shirt and shoes to the table, and you mind your manners.

In the house, you don't swear, and you don't raise your voice for any reason. You clean up after yourself, and you're expected, in her words, "to make a contribution" — just talking about "making a contribution" tires me out. I can barely make it through Sunday night.

It's a wonder that her kids aren't totally screwed up, too — you know, have their creativity stifled and all. That's what Sue says will happen eventually. Sue says they'll go all mental and have breakdowns or just start acting like little robots who can't think for themselves. Maybe she's right.

But as Mrs.-Perfect-Lady-Karen would say, "I've forgotten my manners." I haven't introduced myself. I'm Hank. That's short for Henry Collins, Jr. I'm an average kid in most ways I can think of. There's stuff I like, like the Orioles, my dirt bike, hanging with Jake, and pitching — at least I used to like pitching. I don't like people on power trips. And I don't like school, which sucks big time. This past spring, things really started to go downhill for me there.

Chapter 2

Before I started school last year, the word I heard was that Crowley gets his seventh grade students to learn and remember facts like no other teacher. "His results are simply extraordinary," I heard Miss Castle, our school librarian, say. Crowley taught us American History. You would think that the history of our own country would be interesting. Well, I hung in there until Christmas, but things really bottomed out in the spring. I didn't flunk or anything, because you have to be brain-dead to fail a course at my school, but Mr. Crowley... man-oh-man!

The problem started when I just couldn't stand his boring routines any more. Every night he'd make us read a real short passage from the textbook and then fill in the blanks in this workbook. In class, Crowley reads aloud the passages we read at night, and then he goes over the fill-in-the-blanks questions we did in the workbook the night before. Then he gives us another fill-in-the-blanks sheet and tells us to do it all over again. He collects our papers and grades them while we do deskwork, or, in my case, while I watch Jackie, my classmate, pick his nose for about ten minutes. Then Crowley hands the graded papers back. Class over. Every Friday, he gives this test that's a combination of all the week's fill-in-the-blanks sheets. That's it. That's the whole course. From what I hear, those are some of the very latest teaching techniques. How lame!

In March, I wonder if anybody in all of Crowley's classes has ever gotten one answer wrong on one of his quizzes. So I decide to fill in one blank wrong on purpose. Crowley puts a red "X" mark next to the blank with the wrong answer, and scribbles in the right one. Well, by the end of April, I get five wrong on a single quiz, and by May, I get a full 10 wrong — all on purpose. Crowley never says a word about it — on paper or to me. All I ever get are a bunch of little red "X's."

So I start writing in answers that I think are real amusing, like "Cal Ripken was the general who Roger Clemons surrendered to at the Camden Yards Court House to end the American League War." He doesn't even catch on to what I'm doing, just writes in four little red X's.

By mid-May, I'm so squirmy and itchy and pissed off, sitting in my chair in Crowley's class feels like being tied to an anthill. I shift all around trying to get comfortable, but every time I look up at the clock, only about thirty seconds have gone by. Suffering through his forty-minute class seems to take like a million years. I think it's reasonable for a guy to try not to go completely loony-bin-crazy, so I start to do other stuff to amuse myself.

I carve my name in the desktop, and that gets me sent to the principal's office, which I don't mind 'cause getting out of Crowley's class feels like getting out of jail. But the next time you get sent to the principal's office, you can get suspended or something, and I admit I was real tempted. But getting suspended means that I'd miss English class, and that's the only interesting thing around this whole place. So it's kind of an art to get it right — piss off Crowley just enough to get thrown out of class but not suspended. Sitting in the hall is the best deal of all because I can read what I want there.

I wind up getting a D+ for the year in American History. Jake, who had no answers wrong for the whole year, gets an A+. He says it proves he's a genius and laughs about what an idiot and a bore Crowley is. Jake plays the game real well. He does just what he's supposed to do and doesn't let stuff get to him. I admire that in a way. But I just can't stand it. And I can't do it, either.

And all my classes are pretty nearly as lousy as Crowley's, except English, and I think at first that class is gonna be awful, too.

It's taught by a little round guy named Mr. Finks, who's losing all his hair, but tries to cover-up by combing skinny pieces across the top of his little round head from one ear to the other.

Anyway, he pops in the first day of classes and, without saying a word, drops all his books on the desk, then turns towards us and recites a poem in this sweet, sad, quiet voice. When he's getting close to the end, the whole room is quiet and listening. And right on the last line, his voice has a little catch to it, and I see his eyes go all wet. He's crying! We're all super quiet while he takes off his glasses and wipes his eyes.

When he gets his act together again, he says, "That was a poem Ben Jonson wrote in 1616 about the death of his son Benjamin. We'll be studying great poetry like that this year, and great short stories, too. In this class, you'll learn about love and death and sex and God, and sometimes you won't know which is which. If you'll come with me, we'll laugh and cry and think together. If you choose not to come, I'm sad for you, but maybe you'll make the trip on your own another time."

That night, I'm eating at Mrs.-Perfect-Lady-Karen's house, and Jake and me, we can't wait to let her know all about class with Mr. Finks. We tell her all about his old, beat-up station wagon that back-fires whenever he parks it in the morning. We tell her about his personal grooming. We tell her about him crying in class. I say he's one weird guy, and she gives us one of her little sayings, "Don't judge a book by its cover," and that's the end of the conversation. I hate to admit it, but she's probably right.

Later in the year, in Finks' class, we read Hemingway's *The Old Man and the Sea*. Old Santiago, the main character, loved that big old fish. The more it hurt him, the more he seemed to love it. Then those bastards took it all away from him, but he blamed himself. They were just doing what sharks always do. "I shouldn't have gone so far out," Santiago says. Maybe he's right to blame himself, but he never would have met his fish if he hadn't. I like Santiago, and I like all that baseball stuff in the book about the great DiMaggio. Boy, it's some story, but a tough one, too.

"So who is this Santiago? Who is this fish?" Mr. Finks asks real innocent in class. "What is this sea? The sharks?" So we fight about it all for a while, and he just listens, cleaning his grungy glasses or smoothing his mustache.

We read lots of other good stuff — poetry, stories — and we talk about it all. My favorite book is by a guy named London with the title *Call of the Wild*. That big old lazy dog, Buck, sure gets in touch with his wild side. And Alaska — you can just break out of civilization and go barbarian there. Mr. Finks sees how much I like that book and asks if I want to read a longer, harder book about the wilds of Alaska. I say, "sure," and he gives me his own copy of *Coming Into the Country* by John McPhee. It *is* harder, but God, how can anybody say they've lived without seeing Alaska?

I read it in just two weeks, and decide I'm gonna homestead in Alaska some day, which is what I tell Mr. Finks when I return the book. He gives me another book, *Into the Wild*, by John Krakauer. It's a great story, and more than a little bit scary. Maybe when I go to Alaska, I'll stay close to a town so I don't starve like that kid did in that freezin' school van of his.

Mr. Finks tells us all about a retreat he goes to every August. Teachers and professors from all over the country come to Ligonier, Pennsylvania to discuss just one famous writer. Last summer, it was a British guy named Eliot who wrote this long poem, and another one about somebody he calls Proofrock. Can you picture anyone doing that every summer during their own vacation? Mr. Finks does. Nobody makes him do it. And he even pays for the conference himself. How weird is *that*?!

But I gotta like the guy. His class is the only thing that keeps me from going crazy all seventh grade. Face it, most of the teachers don't seem too clued in. The real problem is that it's just seventh grade. I'm not sure I can think of much that's good about being twelve or thirteen years old. All sorts of embarrassing stuff happens all the time. I don't like talking about it much — but it's a fact — I'm completely out of control.

Let me give you an example. There I am, sitting in math class one day, and for no reason at all I get this giant boner that keeps growing until it's all uncomfortable and cramped sticking down the inside of my pants leg. Real casual, I sort of shift around in my seat and try to edge that thing over so that it'll lay flat on my stomach. I'm comfortable now, but if this hard-on doesn't back off fast, the bell will ring. If I stand up, I'll look like I have this humongous brick sewed into my pants. Well, the bell does ring, and my boner is still there, so I pretend to be asleep, and everybody gets up to leave, giggling at me as I lie there with my head on the desk. Then, while the teacher is explaining to me why I'm such a rude, nasty child, that thing goes away — so my fake nap does the trick. But damn, why do we have to worry about a body part with a mind of its own?

On the very first day of school, I should have known that the seventh grade was going to suck. I get up to brush my teeth and look in the mirror. There's this big zit, the size of an egg, right between my eyes. Unbelievable! I've never seen anybody anywhere with a crater as big and bad as this sucker. It looks like a volcano and sticks out about an inch. I pop and rub and squeeze it, and put some Clearasil on it, and try to see if it'll look better or worse with a Band-Aid. Amazingly, it's a pretty tough decision. With the Band-Aid, I look like a dork. Without it, I look like a Cyclops from another planet. The best plan, I decide, is just to stay home from school, but Sue just laughs at me and says it isn't so bad. I decide I'll go as a one-eye extraterrestrial, but the zit still oozes all day long and every kid stares at it — the teachers too. You can tell when someone is staring at you, and when they're look-ing at something on your face instead of in your eyes. The whole week I'm playing "Mr. Crater Face," that's all people do — stare. And the worst thing is that it happens about every other week all year. Nobody looks as dorky as I do with those humongous oozing craters.

I know this stuff is "supposed to happen" at my age, whatever that means, but that doesn't make it any easier to handle. I grow five inches between the start and end of school. I'm either hungry or tired, or both, all the time. My clothes never fit, so I get these high-water pants and these shirts that have to stay out 'cause the tails are too short and won't stay in. Mrs.-Perfect-lady-Karen hands me some deodorant one weekend and says it's time I start using it every morning after I shower. It's embarrassing when your step-mother has to be the one to tell you something like that.

Meantime, Jake's got this strong, muscular little body, and all his body hair is where it's supposed to be, though I don't know exactly when he got it. I get these gnarly little hairs, one at a time, that turn into these clumps that you can barely see, so I don't want to shower after P.E., or after sports, or anytime 'cause I look like I'm still about five years-old.

As bad as seventh grade was, the summer's not turning out any better. First, Coach keeps making us do all this run-around-the-bases garbage after practice, and I quit. Then, though I've got time to burn, it looks like I'm not going to get down to the beach at all with Sue and Pete. One of these days, I figure, I'm due for a little fun and a little good luck.

Chapter 3

It's the Thursday before the Fourth of July. Jake has a baseball team clinic to get to. Pete and Sue have decided to just hang out at home all weekend. And I've got big plans. When Sue gets home from work today at about 5:30, I'm gonna blow her socks off by showing her a big old gold hoop I got pierced in my left ear. Mrs.-Perfect-Lady-Karen tells Jake if he gets his ear pierced, she'll snatch it right off him. I believe her. So does Jake.

Nancy is the girl who does all the body piercing at our school. I mean, you should see her. Her nose is pierced. So is one eyebrow — with this little tiny gold ring. She's got rows of rhinestone studs in her ears. And she's even pierced her tongue. I used to try to watch her eat in the cafeteria without being too obvious, but I never got a real good angle. I wonder how she manages it. This may sound gross, but I'll bet that whenever she sneezes, she gets snot all over her cheeks because of that nose piercing. To be perfectly honest, Nancy just about scares the snot out of me, but I figure she's an expert. Going to her for my first earring makes a helluva lot of sense.

As it turns out, the piercing doesn't hurt more than a little pinch, and she doesn't charge me since this is my first piercing. She says, real slow, "I don't charge virgins." Nancy has these long, red-brown fingernails, this funny dyed red-brown hair, and this real dark red-brown lipstick. She kinda gives me the creeps and makes me curious at the same time. She claims she's Goth, but she just reminds me of a car wreck that you go by on the Interstate. No matter what you see, it's impossible to turn your eyes away.

Anyway, she has me sit on this swivel piano stool and asks me to turn my head to my right. She stands right in front of me with some alcohol and some cotton and a needle. When she bends over to work on my ear — well, she's wearing this India print halter-top that just opens up, and there's hardly anything between me and her breasts. I'm not sure how to act, so I just sit still and enjoy the view. I've never seen breasts up close before in real life except Sue's — and they don't count. Nancy's are kind of soft and vulnerable looking, like baby rabbits or puppies. They make you want to rub up against them real gentle.

Nancy finishes my ear before I look as much as I want. I give serious thought to having my right ear done just so I can take another look. It's hard to say why I like looking so much.

It's hard to say a lot of things about girls. About two years ago, I gave up pretending I didn't like them, but I don't like how stupid I get around some of them either. Most of the girls I play on teams with or sit in class with don't get me acting that way, but a few of them have started to. And there's no predicting which girls will make me act like a jerk. I have this urge to sniff their hair or lick their neck or do something totally bogus that would brand me "nerd of the year." I figure I'll just stay away from these girls for now to see if my stupidity cures itself or if it's one of those permanent things I'll just have to live with.

After finishing up the piercing at Nancy's, I decide to cycle through Hereford down to the Gunpowder on York Road. I head upstream on the trail all the way to Pretty Boy Reservoir and then back again. That's a good ride. I want to check out the frog pond. Jake and

I first came across it on a bike ride last April, on a real hot Friday after-noon, and I haven't been able to get it out of my mind since.

We had stopped to watch a coupla fishermen when Jake says to me, "Listen."

We sit there quiet for a few seconds before I hear this gurgling, buzzing, sing-songy hum upriver from where we are. "Locusts?" I guess.

"Nah, let's go," says Jake, and off we ride about a hundred yards, where we stop and listen again. The noise is super loud now, and we know for sure it's frogs — tons of 'em. It's Peeper City, man!

We drop our bikes and walk off the trail about sixty or seventy feet. In front of us is this standing water where the Gunpowder must have overflowed from the snow-melt or something. But it isn't a real pond. It doesn't have a muddy bottom, just leaves and rocks and moss like the rest of the woods, with trees and bushes and stumps all through it. It's a little low spot full of water, and the afternoon sun, warm and nice, is shining on the water, and the water's swarming with little tadpoles, big tadpoles with legs, frogs with tails, and full-frogs. All of them are swimming, or splashing, or hopping around.

I know I use big numbers too much, and Mrs.-Perfect-Lady-Karen says I'm gonna lose my credibility if I keep doing it, but I mean there are zillions of frogs sittin' and blinkin' in the sun with just their heads above the water or squattin' on a leaf. The noise is awesome. I musta got 200 frogs rounded up in this little log fort, and Jake got a ton of 'em too. We slop around in the water goin' "ribbit, ribbit" and have a great time.

Finally, we get tired and just sit there and watch. We must be there all afternoon, watching and listening and wondering how all the frogs got there. We can't figure out any explanation that makes us happy. Jake says the power of the sun must just stir things up in the ground, and in the water, and suddenly there's all this new life. That's pretty heavy stuff.

When Jake and me leave the pond, I start to feel sort of sad. What's going to happen to all these little frogs? Raccoons and cats and anything wild that likes frogs will be waiting there for them as soon as it gets dark. I don't think it would be such a nice place at night — all those new frogs with just their little heads pointing out of the water into the moonlight getting eaten, one by one, until they're all gone, after which the woods get real quiet. I wish there was some way to warn the frogs to stay under water — to make those tadpoles, especially, know that getting their heads above water in that place isn't a very sure or easy thing.

I tell Sue all about it when I got home that night, and she just says, "Ick, I hate frogs." Pete isn't too interested either.

I couldn't bring myself to go back until today.

And I have a hell of a time finding the pond again. At first, I think I get it right because in this one low area, the leaves on the ground have a different look to them — sort of older. But the water is all gone, and, on the surface of things, this place is just like any other old place in the woods. I kick up some leaves and lift up some fallen logs, but there isn't even any sign that the frogs had ever been here before. They've just disappeared. I'll come back next year to see if the pond happens again.

By the time I bike back to York Road, it's getting dark. I think I'll take a quick look on the other side of York Road, where there are some pretty parts of the river. That's where I see that chopped-off dude with his baby. She's waving her little rod around from her perch behind his head, and he's moving his rod back and forth so his line loops and straightens before shooting low over the water toward the undercut far bank of the river. I see his rod bend, and he starts reeling in his line while he talks to his baby. "Daddy's got another fish," he says. "It'll be a pretty little brown one with all those spots you like."

The baby gurgles back at him, and he gently picks the fish up out of the water and holds it over his shoulder so the baby can have a look. She focuses right in on that fish, too, and wants to grab it, but her Daddy puts it back into the river and it's gone. "Bye, bye, fishy," he says and the baby waves.

I watch the guy and the baby for another thirty minutes or so, even though it's getting harder to see. They must catch six or eight fish, each time taking turns looking at it and then sliding it back into the water. That's cool.

It takes me most of a half-hour to get home from the river, and I'm beginning to look forward to showing off my new ear, so I cycle pretty hard. When I walk in the front door, I see Sue and Pete sitting cross-legged, facing each other on the living room floor over by the coffee table, which has about six or seven beer cans on it as well as an empty pizza box. They've been smoking their dope again, and the place reeks.

"Hi, Sue. Hi Pete," I say. "Save any pizza for me?"

"Where you been, Hank?" Pete asks. "We ate it all 'cause we did-n't know when you'd get home. And man, it's late, you know." That ole Pete — master of the obvious. You'd never know he's smart, but he must be, 'cause he's some kind of network maintenance guy at an auto parts company. He takes care of all that technical stuff, goin' into the back of computers and makin' the software work with the hard-ware. He likes it, he says, 'cause no one can tell him what to do, and everybody else at the company is basically ignorant about computer stuff. He can tell them almost anything and they'll buy into it as long as things work. The hours are good and so's the pay. He doesn't have to take any shit from anyone. He's got a good gig going, but you'd never know it from the way he's a slug around the house.

I especially don't like the way Sue acts around him either — like she's some kind of real cool retro 60's hippy, which is about as uncool as anything I can think of.

She says to me, "Hi, sweetie. Come on over and give your Mommy a big hug and kiss." I hate it when Sue smokes that stuff 'cause it makes her all sloppy and stupid. Drunks at least know they're drunk, but Sue thinks she's fine when she smokes dope. She says it "mellows her out," makes life "copasetic" for her — whatever that means — and brings out her creative and artsy side. Sometimes she writes poetry when she's smoking. I've read some good poetry. Hers isn't. I go over and give her a hug and a kiss and then escape to the kitchen.

Sue's hard to figure. She meets my real Dad when she's a para-legal at the firm right after she gets outta Goucher College. She's thinkin' maybe she wants to be a lawyer for some good cause some-day and wants to see what the legal stuff's like before goin' to law school. He's older than her, and she says she just fell for him when they had to work real close on some big corporate deal. She's the super-feminist-hippy-crunchy-tree-hugger-type, but she ends up get-ting hitched to this suit. *Go figure.*

Anyway, the marriage doesn't last too long. Sue tells me Dad "couldn't keep his pecker in his pants." I gotta tell you, that's *TMI* — Too Much Information! Anyway, when they get divorced, she has to leave the law firm, and she decides there's no way she's goin' in for all the hassle involved with being in the law. Plus, she has me, which, the way she tells the story, sounds like a major inconvenience. For a while, she just lives on child support from Dad, but then she gets a job as a dispatcher at one of the truck locations in Pete's company. That's where they meet. Right after that, they start goin' out, and get hitched.

Sue says she's rejected the whole establishment thing — that work doesn't tell her who she is. It just pays for the stuff that matters to her. She says that the people on power trips — the workaholic types — are just control freaks, and that they're the ones who've completely screwed up the country.

Sue's got this list of stuff she's said so many times I've got it memorized. It's supposed to mean something real deep, but it sounds more like some kind of code. She says at the front end, "This says it all," and then she recites her little list: "JFK, Bobby, MLK, Tet, My Lai, Cambodia, Watergate, Iran Contra, Whitewater, Travelgate, Monica." Everything runs together like it's all one word.

I'm not sure exactly what she means by all this, except it probably explains the bumper stickers she's got on her old VW — "Question Authority," and "Free Huey," whoever he was. She's like still in the 60's, but there doesn't seem to be anything now she wants to protest. I think she just likes the beach and "mellowing out with her man." That seems to be her thing.

Well, in the kitchen, there isn't much around that looks eatable, but I dig out some Cocoa Crispies and some milk that smells a little bogus but turns out to be OK. There's also a big block of yellow cheese shoved way into the back of the fridge. The outside's a little hard, but the inside's fine. I cut up the cheese and put it on these Ritz crackers with a little slice of sweet pickle. I can feel my mouth getting wet, just thinking about eating my concoctions. I'm so hungry.

That's when Pete comes in and says, "Wow, man, I've got the munchies. What we got out here?" He sees my cheese and crackers, and I tell him it's my entire dinner.

He says, "Don't be so stingy, man," and he takes about seven of them back into the living room for himself. That's almost half of what I got!

Now that really pisses me off, but there's not a thing I can do about it. I can go in and complain to Sue, but she and Pete'd just wind up yelling at each other. I can go out and try to take the stuff back, but Pete would end up hitting me. He's done it before after he's smoked dope. Not hard enough to hurt me much, but hard enough to get Sue screaming and crying, which is not a pretty sight or sound. My only real option is to just be a little hungry, even though that sucks, big time.

I eat my cereal and what's left of my cheese in the kitchen, clean up, and go out into the living room. They're both on the floor staring at the tube. I say I'm going to bed and Sue looks up. "Goodnight, honey," she says.

"Goodnight, Sue," I say.

Neither Sue nor Pete even notices my earring.

Chapter 4

To me, smoking dope or tobacco is no big deal. In fact, I did both last spring, when I was still in the seventh grade. Dad takes Mrs. Perfect-Lady-Karen out for dinner one Saturday night, so Jake and me go to his room to check out the Newports I'd gotten off Pete. We really get stupid together, acting tough in front of the mirror. We hang the cigarettes off our bottom lips and talk so the ash flips around. We flex and wear our hats at weird angles and jump around like Gangster Rappers. Jake turns up Pearl Jam real loud and starts flippin' out on his air guitar. Cracks me up!

We don't do much actual smoking. Mostly we just look in the mirror and act like we're smoking. I do know that if I suck in, it burns and makes me cough. I feel a little sick after a while, so I stop breathing it in. Everybody always makes a big deal out of smoking We have to watch stupid movies at school and go to the most boring health classes in the whole history of boring. I think I can take or leave this stuff.

Well, Perfect-Lady herself knocks on Jake's door at about 10:15 and sticks her head in to say goodnight. She gets this sour expression on her face and asks, "Who's been smoking in here?"

"Not us," I say.

"Jake, come with me," she says, and opens the door wide enough for him to leave. He's gone for about a half an hour.

When he comes back, he says, "I couldn't lie to her. She always knows the truth anyway."

"So what's going to happen?" I ask.

"I dunno," says Jake. "She says I've broken her trust. She doesn't know what she's going to do except tell Dad."

Well, I tell Sue. She says it's no big deal — that Karen, who she can't stand, should chill out. Then at breakfast, Dad gives me his little talk. He tells me that I could have burned down the house, that smoking is bad for me, plus all this other stuff that Mrs. Perfect-Lady-Karen has fed to him.

After a while, Mrs. Perfect-Lady-Karen comes up with the perfect way to make Jake and me miserable. She arranges for us to spend an entire Saturday with this dorky doctor friend of hers who walks us all around Johns Hopkins Hospital. First, we go to a lab, where we put on rubber gloves, and this lab guy hands us this gray-looking thing, which he says is a smoker's lung. Then he hands me a smoker's heart. It's disgusting looking too, but not as bad as the lung. Then he has us hold healthy lungs and hearts that are pink and not so gross looking. You don't have to be Einstein to figure out that there's a big difference.

Then we go up to a floor where they have these old guys lying in beds and hooked up to machines. They're in really bad shape, with tubes up their noses and throats.

One guy's moaning. He has no hair at all. The doctor says he's got emphysema, which he says is like being strangled to death slowly, a day at a time, until one day you finally can't get enough air. Another guy's making these gurgling noises and pawing at the tubes in his face. His eyes are wild, and his gray hair sticks out at weird angles everywhere. The doctor says he's a lung cancer victim. They'd already cut out one of his lungs, but the cancer has already spread too much, even with all the chemical treatments and everything. They're just trying to keep him as comfortable as possible until he dies.

Well, I feel sorry for these guys, but none of that is going to happen to me, and, besides, Mrs. Perfect-Lady-Karen can't tell me that all those millions of smokers out there wind up choking to death in some hospital. On TV, you see old guys with no teeth who live to 100. They've been drinking moonshine and smoking cigarettes for 90 years. Hey, if it's your time, it's your time, and that's all she wrote.

Pete says that these health Nazis just want to tell everybody how to live — that they exaggerate everything just so they can tell you what to do. He says smoking is OK just as long as you don't overdo it. Well, Pete gets out of breath just going up the stairs. He's full of shit about most stuff, but I agree with him on one thing — I don't like people on these power trips telling me how to act.

When I say that to Mrs. Perfect-Lady-Karen, her voice gets real shaky. "I don't want you spreading that poison in my house and hurting the people I love," she says. "If you want to go into a cave by yourself and suck in that nicotine and tar, then I can't stop you, but don't you do it around me or my family. Do I make myself clear?"

"Yes," I say. "You're clear." Mrs. Perfect-Lady-Karen is always clear.

About two weeks after that, I decide to smoke dope for the first time. I'd talked to Jake about it, and he says, "Count me out!" I don't blame him. Seeing Mrs. Perfect-Lady-Karen's reaction to tobacco, she might have a hemorrhage if she finds out that Jake ever tried dope.

I go to the WaWa parking lot with Nancy and some of the other kids who are big into grunge and skateboarding. They wear these really baggy clothes, speak in code, and have these hand signals and stuff. Most of these kids are OK, but they're pissed off at school, their parents, and life in general. They pass around a couple of joints. I have eight or nine hits and start to feel pretty strange. I get on my bike and start to ride home, but I'm sweating really heavy and feel a little dizzy. I stop to rest and feel too weird to get back on the bike. It takes me a while to feel better. Maybe that stuff just doesn't agree with me now, but I don't see what the big deal is. Then again, if it makes you as stupid and sloppy as it does Pete and Sue, then that's not so hot either.

I tell Jake all about it. He's real interested and asks me all sorts of questions. We pretty much decide that we have enough problems without dope right now, and don't need something else we have to worry about.

Maybe I'll give it a try some other time. We'll see.

Chapter 5

During the school year, we load our tired selves every Sunday into Karen's Voyager van and drive a half hour to St. George's Episcopal Church on Garrison Road. But usually we get out of church during summers. One Saturday night at dinner, Jake gives the Perfect-Lady a rash, which, most times, he can do without her going off on him.

"God is dead," he says, repeating the words of a bumper sticker we both saw peeling off an orange VW Camper from the '60s.

She rises to the bait. "Where do you get such nonsense, Jake?"

Jake winks at me. "Well, Mom," he says, "you tell us about all that bad stuff in Bosnia, and you talk all about the Palestinians. God's supposed to be good, so he sure wouldn't let all that happen if he were alive, would he?"

Well, I can tell from the look on her face that Mrs. Perfect-Lady-Karen is winding up for a pretty stiff lecture, so I pipe up and try to cut her off before she gets started. "He's not dead," I say. "He's on vacation, just like us. He only pays attention when school's on. During the summer, he goes fishin'."

Mrs. Perfect-Lady-Karen says nothing and, with a far away look on her face, starts to eat her corn on the cob. Even the way she eats corn is weird — not back and forth, down the rows, like everybody else, but round and round. And even though she picks every cob clean, I've never seen her get any kernels stuck in her teeth. The rest of us have to pick away at all that junk, but not her. Anyway, I know that look. It usually means she's thinking, and that never comes to any good.

We're loading up the dishwasher when it finally pops out. "We're all going to church tomorrow," she says. Damn!

Up in his room, Jake tells me, "Don't make the grown-ups feel guilty, man. They're likely to act on it. I just wanted to stir her up a little, but, Jesus, Hank, you had to go and make her think about why we don't go to church in the summer." Jake's right. I didn't think it through. I never should have opened my fat mouth!

So off we go. The church building, which is worn-out brick and wavy glass windows, is OK. Big oak trees hang over it. To get inside, you have to walk through a graveyard full of old markers with worn down names you can hardly read. I like one that stands all crooked, with a skull and wings on it, near the church door. The marker was probably white once, but now it's splotchy gray-green. The guy under there is "William Oliver McHenry Lewiston, Jr. BORN July 9, 1789, DIED January 3, 1842."

Right next to that marker is a little bitty tilted one. You have to get down on your hands and knees to read it. It says, "William Oliver McHenry Lewiston III, BORN March 19, 1821, DIED February 26, 1826." It makes me think of Mr. Finks and his Ben Jonson poem.

Inside the church are thick, whitewashed walls with a few yellowy cracks going up and down like ivy vine. The warped glass windows are set a few feet back into the old walls, and make the trees and clouds look all wavy and fuzzy. Sometimes they turn green into purple, or add rainbow streaks to the sky. The pews by the aisle are white on the sides, except for finger marks and hand smudges on the dark tops.

The seats are dark brown and polished from lots of butts sliding over them to make room for the people running in late. The late-comers are sorta slouched over, and tip-toe across the bricks. They look kinda embarrassed, but they also look pleased to be noticed.

Ladies' high heels make a hell of a clatter on those red bricks, and last winter a woman with chicken legs tore her shoe off in the old iron-floor grating halfway up the aisle. She tried to yank the thing out with her hands, but it was stuck good, and it sat there for the whole service like a giant old cat turd on a rock. All the choir people gave it a neat sidestep on their way out, and the minister, before *he* stepped over it, gave it a look like he smelled something bad. After the service, I got the shoe out for the lady by giving it a hard twist, and she said thanks. I said to her, "No, ma'am, thank you!" She made the whole service entertaining.

Well, the service on this miserable hot Sunday in late July has the potential for complete disaster. They're baptizing some kid, and they're also doing a communion during the same ceremony, which means we might die of old age before we ever see the sunlight again. Even worse, it's one of those heavy days when you feel like somebody just threw a steaming horse blanket on top of you and you're gonna be smothered to death. Everybody's fanning themselves, in spite of the three electric fans set up around the altar. The ladies have big wet splotch marks under their arms and on their dresses, and all the men have wet collars.

God's paying attention, though, and he saves me from the boredom and gets my mind off the heat. It's Mr. Finks' baby who's getting baptized today! I didn't know he was a member of this church, but there he is, uncomfortable as usual, shifting from foot to foot with a wet piece of hair hanging down over one ear almost to his shoulders. Who woulda guessed he'd find somebody to marry — and then to have a kid with? GEEZ!

While he's wiping his smudged glasses, I can barely keep myself from yelling, "Hey, Mr. Finks. It's me, Hank!" Instead, I just jab Jake in the ribs with my elbow until he sees, and he says, "Holy shit... how about that... and look there, his wife is kinda cute." She is, too, a short woman in a blue, low-cut sun-dress and a head full of straw-colored hair, under a floppy hat with a broad brim and a red ribbon. I stare down the aisle and see her holding her baby. Mrs. Finks has a nice set of knockers, too!

Mr. Finks stands next to her in a yellow bow tie and one of those wrinkled blue and white striped numbers he usually wears to school. He looks pretty darn good, too, given natural limitations.

Church services usually don't do much for me. In fact, I don't remember ever listening too hard to them. But some stuff sticks in my mind, like what Mrs.-Perfect-Lady-Karen calls the "Good Night Prayer." During today's service, that prayer, for some reason, is rattling around in my head:

O Lord, support us all the day long, until the shadows length-en and the evening comes, and the busy world is hushed, and the fever of life is over, and our work is done. Then in thy mercy grant us a safe lodging, and a holy rest, and peace at the last.

I don't know why that whole thing sticks with me because my brain only holds bits and pieces of other prayers — you know, the ones we say all the time, like, "We have erred, and strayed from thy ways like lost sheep... and there is no health in us," or something like that. Or that other one, which no one can ever forget: "Glory to the Father, and to the Son, and to the Holy Ghost. As it was in the beginning, is now, and ever shall be, world without end. Amen."

Anyway, the minister starts off by saying that today he is honoring an unusual request. It seems that language is particularly important to the Finks family, and the church is honoring its special request to use the unrevised "Ministration of Holy Baptism" from the *1928 Book of Common Prayer*. None of that means much to me, except Finks must have made some kind of ruckus, and if he held out for it, it probably ain't too bad. They hand out special copied sheets so we can follow the service, and now I'm curious to see what's up.

It starts pretty well. The minister calls us his "Dearly beloved," which is new to me, and then he says the kid, who is just beginning to squirm and wail, is gonna be baptized with "water and the Holy Ghost." No wonder the kid's nervous!

Then the minister asks the members of the congregation, who are the innocent bystanders in this whole deal, if we "in the name of the child, renounce the devil and all his works, the vain pomp and glory of the world, with all the covetous desires of the same, and the sinful desires of the flesh?"

Yikes! I practically see the devil about to jump off the balcony — this is classic Finks stuff, all right. But the best part is when the minister takes the baby, who looks bright pink in the face and as limp as an overcooked string bean, and washes his head while calling him by name — Ebenezer O'Hara Finks (what a friggin' name that is!).

Then, with his thumb, the minister outlines the sign of the cross on the baby's little pink forehead. The part that kills me, the part that I can't forget, is when the minister says, "We receive this child into the congregation of Christ's flock; and do sign him with the sign of the Cross, in token that hereafter he shall not be ashamed to confess the faith of Christ crucified, and manfully to fight under his banner, against sin, the world, and the devil; and to continue as Christ's faithful soldier and servant unto his life's end." Who wrote that stuff? It practically gives me goose bumps.

And who could ever forget this picture: a little kid, with his pink face all wrapped in white, alongside his hairy, sweating father, who can't see much through dirty lenses, standing next to his hot little wife with the nice rack, and the minister in white and black and green? Geez, what a mix of the funny, the odd, and maybe the powerful. You'd think Finks is trying to continue his English classroom right here in the church.

But there's one more picture, and this one just about makes the whole summer. After the baptism, when most of us are sweaty and pretty close to tears, we have to sit through the whole "body and blood" routine. That fat little fart Harvey Walters, the acolyte, has been up there on the altar throughout the service, his broad ass cool as a cucumber because he's sitting in front of those three electric fans. Now it's his job to help out the minister mixing and carrying around stuff.

Well, Harvey does it. He walks right smack in front of one fan carrying a full, wide-open box of those nasty little round wafers that stick to the roof of your mouth, that you gotta scrape off with your finger. Before fat Harvey can do much, those wafers are flying everywhere. It looks like it's snowing, and now Harvey, who, like us, is starting to sweat, is trying to grab the flying wafers, and he's missing. The minister just freezes, and then the whole congregation just laughs out loud. I think I'm gonna shit a brick I laugh so hard. Even Mrs.-Perfect-

Lady-Karen cracks a smile.

Poor old Harvey! Good old Mr. Finks! In St. George's Church, Garrison Road, Owings Mills, Maryland that Sunday in July, we were all dodging wafers while fighting the temptation of the devil. It was rich, I'll tell you that much.

Chapter 6

Finally, I've got something good to do this summer. Dad's reserved his law firm's box at Camden Yards, and Jake and I are going for an Orioles game. All the local dinosaurs say that watching the O's at this fancy stadium sucks because the Yuppies have taken over. They say Memorial Stadium had a special feeling and everybody could afford to go. They talk about section 34 in the upper deck where a crazy man named Wild Bill Hagey got everybody going by spelling out O-R-I-O-L-E-S with his body. They say the O's were more fun when Brooks and Frank Robinson, Boog Powell, Paul Belanger, Paul Blair, and Earl Weaver were on the team.

Well, maybe they're right. I can't say 'cause I'm not as old and worn out as those people. I do know that Cal Ripken is the best baseball player in the world, and that Brady Anderson is as good a lead-off hitter and outfielder as we've ever had. So screw all the old timers. Let 'em stay home if they think going to the Yard sucks. That leaves more room for me and Jake.

I only got to sit in the firm box once before. Usually, I'm up in the nosebleed sections or out in the bleachers. It doesn't matter where you sit when the game starts 'cause you can always sneak down to the good seats in the late innings. But these seats are great. They're behind the visiting team's dugout, about three rows back on the third base side. You can look right into the Orioles' dugout, too, and see what's going on in there, and you can talk to the players on the other team, if you want to. Last time I was in these seats, I was pretty little — eight or something — but I remember we were playing the Yanks, and Wade Boggs said "hi" and smiled at us. *Wade Boggs!*

Me and Jake take the light rail downtown for tonight's game. The Perfect-Lady-Karen drops us off at the station, but only after making us change out of our T-shirts and put on clean pants. "You don't want to embarrass your father, Hank," she says. "You'll be sitting with nice people."

I say screw her, but it isn't worth fighting about, so I just give her the sour look that drives her nuts, and then the silent treatment all the way to the station. "Have fun and be good," she says. *Yeah, right.*

We get on the light rail car in Lutherville, and it takes about a half hour or so to get all the way downtown. There are other people heading down for the 7:30 game as early as us. Mostly they're men. A lot of 'em wear Orioles gear and talk baseball.

One dad is trying to keep his bratty little kid, who has some kind of food all over his face, from pressing the stop button on the side of the car. The kid's squirming and pushing his father's arms away, but the dad just keeps holding him, saying nothing and looking out the window like he wishes he's somewhere else. The mother just sits there like a troll, chewing gum and saying nothing. Every once in a while, she pops her gum, and looks startled, like the sound woke her up from wherever she was. When she looks over at her man and the squirming kid, she looks like she doesn't know them. Then she goes back to chewing and staring out the window.

We get off at the Pratt Street stop and walk over to a bar/restaurant called "Pickles." That's where fraternity boys from Towson or Hopkins or Loyola hang out before games, and where a kid at school says they'll give you a beer if you ask right. We mix with the college crowd on the sidewalk because most of them can't fit inside.

Little kids holding their fathers' hands push through the sidewalk crowd, and blue-haired old ladies dressed in Orioles black and orange hold their purses tight against their chests, trying to get by the beer drinkers without getting wet or knocked down. Young guys in twos or threes talk real loud about who's gonna win tonight as they dip out into traffic instead of fighting through the sidewalk mess. Boyfriends and girlfriends walk holding hands, so the boy sort of has to walk ahead, pushing through the beer drinkers, with the girl trailing behind like she's on a leash or something. I like the feel of the place — the noise and the smell, the fact that everybody's going to the game, and is happy to be there. They're all talking loud, smoking cigarettes, hoping the O's can do it again tonight. I can even smell the dogs from the stadium, and Boog's BBQ smoke makes my mouth water.

I walk up to one guy with a beard and an Orioles' jacket. He's smoking a cigarette and standing right by the door of "Pickles." His glass is empty, and he's going in for a refill. "Will you get me a beer, Mister?" I ask him in my politest voice.

He turns around and looks me up and down. "Get lost, you little turd," he says, "or I'll call the cops on you." He turns and goes in.

Jake goes up to a guy — a clean-cut frat type in one of those alligator shirts. He's talking to another guy who's dressed and looks just about the same — khaki shorts, sandals, and shirt, and hair parted on the side. Both these young guys are smoking big cigars and drinking a beer. "Excuse me, sir," Jake says, "but me and my friend here are thirsty and we could use a coupla brewskis to take the edge off." (He musta learned how to talk like that from some commercial.)

Both the cigars laugh at us, and one, who takes a long drag and blows the smoke in our direction, says, pretty sarcastically, "So the little men are out for a night on the town. How'd you shake loose from Mommy and Daddy? I'll get you a beer. Who am I to stand in the way of progress? What's your brand, little man?"

"Bud," Jake says.

"Give me a five," the cigar says, and when Jake does, he turns in a cloud of smoke to go to the bar. A few moments later, he's back with our beers.

"Here you go, little men. Enjoy, stay the hell away from us while you drink these things, and remember: We've never seen you before."

"Thanks," we both say and walk off with our beers. Those two guys are real assholes, but they're our assholes, and the beer tastes great. We sit on the edge of the sidewalk and watch everybody hurrying past. What a perfect night this is going to be!

We drain the last of our beers and leave the bottles on the sidewalk. If we're gonna catch any of batting practice, we're going to have to move it. I feel a little funny as we head into the stadium — not sick exactly, just a little spacey.

Two players send a couple of batting practice shots into the right field bleachers, and one tall fan with bad zits and an amazingly great glove pulls both of 'em in. He hops over seats and races up and down aisles quick as hell. Jake and me are laughing like crazy. We're only about five rows away when the two balls land in the bleachers, but we don't even get close to grabbing them. Oh, well!

We watch Orlando Merced, Toronto's right fielder, as he makes some hard catches look easy, but we can't get him to toss us a ball. He's a fast-looking guy, and, like water over rocks, he seems to flow across the grass like the surface of the Gunpowder over the bottom — natural, easy, fast, effortless, like it's supposed to happen.

We hang around the bleachers for a while before heading to our great seats, which are down the third base line near the dugout. Everybody's happy before a baseball game — even the guy who takes our tickets and wipes off our seats. Jake gives him a dollar, and so do I. That's what Dad says you do for the guy who's got to wipe bird shit off of seats for a living. I could take a load of bird shit and smile like a cheerful idiot all night long if I got to watch every O's game at the Yard.

We watch the ground crew wet down the field and fix up the lines around home plate. A country western singer does the National Anthem, but she can't hit the high notes, so she fakes it by going low instead, and we all scream "O" as loud as we can when she gets to the "Oh say does that star-spangled banner yet wave…" part — that's a good Baltimore tradition, I think.

As we get ready for the top of the first, everything's great, except Dad hasn't shown up yet, and four dudes about three rows behind us have already spilled their beer down this old lady's back. They're saying real loud that they're sorry, but they're laughing while they say it. One guy drops his nachos and cheese, and his friend steps right in it. They all laugh like hell.

One guy's wearing a cap marked "Callahan's Demolition" on the front, and another, his cigarettes rolled up in the sleeve of his T-shirt, is smoking a cigarette, which pisses off the guy behind him. The third dude is spitting tobacco juice into a plastic beer cup. An usher comes down and tells them to put out the cigarettes, which the dudes don't like. When a beer guy comes down the aisle, all four of them buy two beers apiece. I think they've already had six. I turn around and watch, because, though the four are noisy and smiling and funny at first, there's something about them that I don't want to get too near.

Just as the first inning ends — with the O's hitting into a double play — Dad finally shows up, still dressed in his dark suit and tie. His client looks like a business clone. Why do men go to the ballpark in suits? Why don't they change? In fact, why do they go to these games at all? Maybe they feel important in their starched white shirts and their suspenders showing. Holding their suit coats in their laps, they look hot and stiff and uncomfortable, and most of them don't pay attention to the game, just like Dad doesn't. He says "hi" to us and introduces us to "Mr. Markham," and then the two of them get a beer and start to talk. Just about then I hear one of the jerks behind us say, "Who's this guy on deck? What kind of a name is that … MERKD?"

Then one yells out, "Hey, MERKD, what the hell kind of name is that?" They're talking about Orlando Merced.

Then, as Merced goes up to bat, one of the smart guys notices that Merced's name is on the scoreboard. "Look there, that boy's name is Orland-o MERKD." Then he yells, "Hey, Or-land-ooh, are you a nigger or a spic? Looks like yo' mama couldn't make up her mind."

Then they all howl with laughter. I watch Merced, and can tell he hears them. His back sort of stiffens up. That's a load of crap, talking like that. I turn to Jake and can tell he doesn't like it either. He says real low to me, "That guy needs to have his ass kicked."

"Yeah," I say, turning around to look at them again. Everybody in the section is sort of looking and mumbling, but they don't do anything. I turn to Dad and elbow him to get his attention. "Did you hear that?" I say.

Dad nods and says, "They're real jerks. Just ignore them."

But then Merced strikes out, and he's walking back to the Toronto dugout when one of 'em yells, "Hey, Or-Laaand-oooh, you're a nigger and you're a spic and you can't hit worth a shit — that's three strikes and you're back to Porta Rica!" Again they all laugh like hell, and Merced gives a quick little look up into the stands before he drops out of sight into the dugout.

Now that really pisses me off. I grab Dad by the arm, and say, "Dad, you gotta do something about those guys!"

He leans toward me and, without looking back, says, "It's none of our business what those guys say. They paid for their tickets same as we did, so they can say what they want." Then he turns back to talk to his business clone.

I say to Jake, "Somebody ought to shut those assholes up," and Jake nods. His face gets splotchy, like it always does when he's angry, but this time he says nothing.

To finish out the inning, the O's pitcher strikes out the third Toronto batter, and then, when we're back at bat, we smack a home run! But I can't enjoy the game. The animals behind us are making a lot of noise, and now they're ordering more beers.

In the top of the fifth, Orlando comes back out of the dugout to bat and I hear from behind me, "Hey, nigger boy, did your spic momma sleep with some nigger sailor?" The four dudes laugh, and Merced doesn't turn around, but again he's looking kind of stiff and mechanical. He hears them. I know it. Again, I look at my father, and again he just looks straight ahead. He hears, too, but he's just gonna sit there. I look over for Jake, but he's gone to the bathroom or some- thin'. This whole thing sucks, and it looks like nobody's gonna do jack-shit about it. So I jump up onto my seat, looking big as I can, and scream at the top of my lungs, "Why don't you jerks shut up and leave Orlando alone?"

I've never heard a ballpark get so quiet so quick. For just a few seconds, it seems like everybody just freezes in place, like when you hit pause on the videotape. Dad's grabbing at me to sit down, but I'm standing there, stiff, feeling like I'm gonna cry, which would be really embarrassing. My face is all hot, and I've got my fingers all curled up into fists. I know I'm starting to shake, and I can't sit down.

Then the dude with the demolition cap stands up and yells, "Hey, you nigger lovin' little punk, why don't you come on up here?"

I can't think of anything to say at first and Dad's yanking at me and telling me to turn around and sit down, but then I yell, "Just shut your fat mouth so we can watch the game."

That's when the big guy says, "Why, you little asshole," and he starts to climb across his friends to get to the aisle. I'm too pissed off to be scared, but I know I'm in some deep shit now.

Thank God for Jake. He comes running down the aisle with an usher and two Baltimore cops. They get there just as the demolition cap guy stumbles over his friend's feet and into the aisle, nearly knocking down the usher. The demolition guy straightens up and sees the cops, but he takes a step down the aisle toward me anyway. One cop takes out his club and stands in the way. Then there's some yelling and some cussing, and the four guys all get up and start up the aisle, and both cops follow them. They turn and look at me.

One guy gives me the finger. Another one says, "We're coming back for you!" But they leave, and everyone around is standing up and watching them go. A bunch of people around us start to clap, and pretty soon everybody in the section is clapping.

As I sit down, I feel like I'm going to puke. Jake's face is still all splotchy, but he's smiling at me, and the usher comes down to shake Jake's hand. "Good job, son," he says, looking at me and at Dad. "You've got some good boys there, Mister."

A guy behind me pats me on the shoulder, and a guy in front

turns around and says, "You got guts, kid."

Now I'm feeling a bit better, but I'm still not great. Dad says, "You got real lucky there, Hank. All of us could have gotten hurt."

"Not *him*," I think to myself. "He'd have pretended not to know me." All those people clapping and saying nice things about me did nothing. I don't get it. Those four guys were screwing up the whole baseball game and everybody in my section just sat there with their thumbs up their butts. It took Jake to do the right thing, and he's only thirteen.

After a few more innings, I calm down a little. The Orioles' second baseman goes to his right and makes a great stop on a grounder up the middle, leaping into the air, and throwing across his body to rob Toronto of an easy single. But our pitching looks tired, and one Toronto batter, with one man on, ropes a high curve ball into the left field stands to tie up the game at two apiece. The Orioles manager comes out. I figure he's gonna call in a reliever. That's when Dad and his business clone decide to leave. "I've got more work to do back at the office tonight," Dad says. "Just take the light rail to Lutherville and call Karen to pick you up. I'll let her know to expect your call. I'll need an hour or more to wrap things up."

"OK," we say, though we'd been looking forward to the car ride home, with the windows down and the radio up. Hell, the light rail's fine if we have to take it.

For a lousy hour or two of work, Dad misses some great pitching. Our first reliever mows 'em down for two innings, then short relief comes in and blows Toronto away during the top of the ninth. But we can't score, and here we are, still tied, in the top of the tenth. We walk one, but we get a double play.

We do nothing at the plate, and in the eleventh the manager

brings in a new Orioles reliever. He makes the Blue Jays look stupid for two innings, which puts us in the bottom of the twelfth. Anderson leads off with a single and is standing on third after we execute a perfect hit-and-run. Then we strike out, get a walk, and hit a deep sacrifice fly to plate the winning run. Jake and I yell ourselves stupid. What a great game!

Instead of fighting our way through the crowd to get onto the light rail, I say to Jake that the game lasted a long time and maybe Dad's finishing up and we can catch a ride home with him. So we run down Pratt Street over to Hopkins Plaza and into the lobby of Dad's office building. The guard would've called ahead for us, but he's catching some major Z's, so we just hit the elevator button for the 18th floor and head up ourselves. We've been here before a coupla times to meet Dad with Perfect-Lady-Karen — once before going over to the Barnum and Bailey Circus, and once when we visited the Aquarium together, so we know our way around pretty good.

When we get to the firm lobby, Jake heads off to take a leak while I go in the other direction to get to Dad's office. The place is spooky, dark, and quiet. Only those little emergency lights and a few desk lamps are on. I jog down the hallway looking in each open door as I go. Dad's office is at the end of the hall, around the corner, but when I get there, his door is closed, with some light coming through the crack underneath. I think I'll scare him, so I turn the knob real quiet and open the door about three inches to peek in.

I wish I'd never opened that door. We should've just taken the light rail home, the way we were supposed to.

Dad is there all right. His pants are down around his ankles, and his white butt is going back and forth, his shirttail slopping around. He's holding onto the hips of this woman with long black hair who's kind of lying there on his desk, her legs bent up high near his chest, her head thrown back. Both are making noises.

I see all this in about five seconds. After closing the door quietly, I start to run back down the hall, where Jake almost runs into me. "What's the rush?" he asks.

"This place gives me the creeps," I say, not bothering to stop. "Let's catch the rail."

"He's left already?"

"Yeah, he's gone."

I punch the elevator button, but I'm about to explode, so I say to Jake, "I'll beat you down."

"No way," he says. So while he takes the elevator, I start down the stairs. He's waiting for me at the bottom, and though I'm out of breath, I don't stop running. "Race you to the station," I pant, taking off for Pratt Street. Jake runs with me, and I'm trying not to cry, and I'm trying to think, and I know I can't think clearly.

Now I know somehow that I can't tell Jake. What would he do if he knew? Would he tell his mother? Would he lie to her by saying nothing? If she knows that Dad is getting his rocks off with some woman down at the office, Perfect-Lady-Karen will walk right out on him, or, more likely, throw him out. Then maybe they'd all move away. I don't want any of those things to happen 'cause I'd never get to see Jake or Stephie again.

All the way home on the train, I act stupid, making noises like I'm a deaf mute. Jake says that I'm not funny — that I'm doing mean stuff we stopped doing in fourth grade. He gets pissed off and stares out the window.

I'm just trying not to cry.

Chapter 7

I toss and turn all night. When Jake's alarm goes off in the morning, I pretend to be asleep. He has to be at the ball diamond for a tournament by nine. Dad's taking him to the game and then going into "work." Ha!

After Jake's gone, I go downstairs to scout out some breakfast. The Perfect Lady is pulling stuff out of the dishwasher, and Stephie is coloring with crayons at the kitchen table.

"Hi, Hank," Stephie says. "What color is a Porky Pine?"

"Pork-U-pine," says the Perfect Lady.

"Brown," I say, before sticking my head into the fridge. I find the OJ carton, which is almost empty, and start to drink it down, but I can feel "the stare" boring into the side of my head like a laser. I turn and say, all innocent, "What?"

"You know," says Karen.

So I close the fridge and, from the cupboard, pull out a glass still hot from the dishwasher. I pour the OJ into the glass, but, as I expect, get only about two inches' worth. That's gone in one gulp, so I toss the carton into the trash and leave the glass on the counter before heading toward the back door. But I can feel the laser again.

"*What?*" I say, this time with more of a whine.

"You know."

"I threw the carton in the trash."

"The glass?"

"You were the one who wanted me to use the stupid glass. It's dirty because you wanted it dirty. That's not my fault."

"Hank, we clean up after ourselves in this house, and besides, I need to talk to you."

There isn't really a choice here. I can start World War Three by going out the door, or I can wash, dry, and put away the glass. My energy feels a little low, so I shuffle over to the glass, run some cold water over it, give it a half-assed wipe with a paper towel, which I know she thinks is a waste when a perfectly good dish towel is hanging above the sink, and put the glass upside down in the wrong cupboard, which drives her nuts. Then I sit down opposite Stephie with my head down on the table, all slouched over.

The Perfect-Lady never takes her eyes off me, but she says nothing. Her energy must be a little low today, too. If she only knew that I had a nuclear payload on board and that I could drop that sucker right there in the kitchen and blow her sorry skinny ass right out the oven ventilator hood. But I look at Stephie coloring and I can't bring myself to do it.

The Perfect-Lady says she's got a million errands to run — the cleaner, the groceries, the hardware store. Pictures need to be developed. The car needs a visit to Jiffy Lube, and she needs to get an engagement gift for some friends from a million years ago. I tune most of it out, but I get the gist. She needs me to stay home with Stephie since Dad and Jake are both gone all day.

I take my fun where I find it. "Shit!" I scream at her. "Why is it always me? Why am I always the one who has to do this or do that? What are you punishing me for?" I go on like this for a coupla minutes, almost convincing myself that I'm super pissed. Really, I just want to get to her.

You gotta give the Perfect Lady credit, though. She just waits me out without changing her face. When I'm done, she stands there quiet for a second. "Alright, Hank," she says, "poor Stephie can come with me. I'll drag her from place to place and she'll have a miserable day. Is that what you want?"

She's got me, and she knows it. I'm tempted for the second time in that short morning to drop my nuclear payload, but I look over at Stephie, still coloring, and I can't do it. I've still got no balls.

"No," I say.

"Alright then," she says. "I'll be back as fast as I can, and absolutely no later than two. Please stay on the property. Call the neighbors if there's a problem. They're home all day. I checked."

The Perfect Lady leaves, and I slump down at the kitchen table to watch Stephie color her Porky Pine bright pink. "Atta girl, Steph," I think to myself. She does things her way — just like Jake does. Neither of them makes much noise about it, so they don't catch much flak. I'm workin' on doing the same, but it's not natural for me.

The pink tip of Stephie's tongue peeks out between little pursed lips. Her straight brown hair is pulled back from a round fore-head and held tight by a rubber band and a barrette. Her wide blue eyes focus on the page.

"Why pink?" I ask her.

"Porky's a pig, and pigs are pink, silly."

"Oh," I say.

She sighs, puts down her crayon, and cocks her head to one side. "Porky's done," she says. "Wanna ride bikes?"

Out to the garage we go. Her little red bike has training wheels and a banana seat. There's a little bell on it and streamers on the handlebars. I had a bike just like it once, but it bit the dust when Dad backed over it on the way to work one dark morning.

"Where's your helmet, Steph?" I ask her.

"I'm not wearing one 'cause *you're* not wearing one," she says.

She's got me there. So I start rummaging through the junk shelves in the garage. I find a helmet, all moldy, that I have to shake a few bug corpses out of, and it sits on the back of my head like a shrunken beanie, and I can't fasten it.

"You look funny, Hank," she giggles at me as I come out of the garage, but my helmet seems to satisfy her and she puts hers on.

We decide to have a motor-bike race — around the house twenty times — and it takes forever because Stephie calls time-out every coupla laps for a bathroom break, or for a commercial time-out, or 'cause "it's-not-fair-that-your-bike's-bigger-and-I-need-a-bigger-headstart" time-out. I ride behind her shouting "vroom-vroom" and pretending to pass her. She veers back and forth to cut me off, looking over her shoulder, and shouting, "Get back, you! Hank, get back, you!"

We finish in a tie, but Stephie wins on what she calls a "techno-calty." Since her bike is smaller, and her wheel doesn't stretch as far, she says, she would have been ahead at the finish line if her bike would have been bigger. *Whatever*!

Now it's time for peanut butter and jelly — with no jelly. Stephie won't call it plain-old peanut butter. It has to be "peanut butter and jelly and no jelly." Don't ask me why. It makes her happy.

We eat our sandwiches and drink lemonade together at the kitchen table. She's all sweaty. Little beads cling to her upper lip, and to the fine little frizzy hairs at her hairline, and sweat is smeared near her temple, onto her forehead, and onto her cheeks. She's flushed, as pink as her Porky Pine, making those wide eyes under her thick eyebrows even bluer.

She looks at me unblinking and asks, "Hank, are you angry?"

"No, Steph, I'm not angry."

"You seem mad. Are you mad at me?"

"I'm never mad at you, Steph," I say.

"At Mommy?"

"I'm mad at your Mommy sometimes, but not now."

"I don't like you to be angry, Hank. You look sad and grouchy like Oscar the Grouch."

"I like Oscar the Grouch!" I say.

"Me too," she says, "but that's because he's funny and lives in a trash can and he's pretend. He wouldn't be funny if he was real, 'cause he'd smell bad."

"Yeah," I agree.

"You wanna play dolls with me? You can be Ken."

"OK," I say, and for the next hour we are a happily married couple racing NASCAR together as a team. Every race, Barbie beats Ken by a whisker, but he tries hard, and as a team they're always champions.

I got lucky today. I got a chance to be alone with Stephie. She likes me even if she has no idea why. I don't know what it would take to make her *not* like me. When I spend time with her, I feel better about stuff. With Stephie, I calm down and relax, and I can be me. I don't have to be what someone else wants me to be. Stephie always says just what she thinks, straight out — no B.S. I wonder when we older people all start being fakes.

Being able to play alone with Stephie also keeps me from saying something stupid. Twice this morning I nearly let loose on the Perfect-Lady, and that would have been a disaster. If she ever thought my father was cheating on her, she'd throw him out of the house quicker than quick. He'd be out, which means I'd be out, too, and, in that case, I might never get to see Jake or Stephie. Karen already thinks I'm a pain the neck. If she tossed Dad out, there'd be no reason for her to let me stay, or even to visit.

So, I can't say a thing to anyone. *Ever.* Stephie is so nice, so happy. She trusts us all, even me, and I don't want that to end, and I don't want me to not see her and Jake. It really gets me, though. Because I can't say anything about his extra-office business, Dad's going to get away with it. They won't know he's a liar. He sits there reading his newspaper, pretending to be somebody he's not. Karen waits on him. Jake admires him. And Stephie loves him. But I know he's an asshole, and a real shit.

Chapter 8

Just like she said she would, the Perfect Lady returns before 2:00 — in fact, with 15 minutes to spare. I see her coming, and time it so I'm leaving just as she's pushing through the kitchen screen door with her bags.

"Where are *you* going?" she asks.

"Out," I say. "On my bike."

"Dinner's at 7:00," she reminds me. "If you want some, be here by then."

I say nothing, get on my bike, and leave. My bike is where I do my best thinking, and the Gunpowder is my favorite place to ride, so I head toward that old, dried-out pond — the one with all the frogs. It always seems like the place I steer toward when my mind's all muddled.

I know I have to keep my mouth shut. "Mouth shut, mouth shut, mouth shut." I say it in my head, over and over, to the rhythm of my pedaling. But soon it changes: "Mouth shut, liar! Mouth shut, liar!" Then, finally, it turns into just, "Liar, liar, liar on a bike tire. Liar, liar, liar, on a bike tire."

Where the frog water was, I lay my bike down, and sit on a downed log, breathing hard and still saying to myself, "Liar, liar, bicycle tire."

And that, unfortunately, reminds me of an incident that happened at school this past spring. I tell old Crowley I have to take a dump. It's another way to kill the boredom. He gives me a hall pass, so off I go and sit down in the stall at the end, nearest the wall. Bingo! I hit it big! In this same stall, I notice, some kid had recently started drawing a big old honker of a penis, and must have gotten startled or stopped because his drawing is only about three quarters done. But he's left his drawing device — a black magic marker — right there on the floor.

I drop my pants down around my ankles and finish off the drawing, adding to it a big old pair of hairy balls. The friggin' marker is leakin' all over the place, though, and it's becoming a pretty messy business for me. Then, I think, this humongous old dick needs a proper name, so I write C-R-O-W-L-E-Y in big block letters the length of the shaft.

Then I think, "What's a great big old dick like Crowley doing without a suitable target?" So I draw in two big thighs spread wide. I give the snatch a name, too — M-I-L-L-E-R. He's our principal and I figure he's been taking it up the wazoo from Crowley, 'cause how else do you explain a boring guy like Crowley being allowed to stay a teacher all these years?

Well, I just finish when I hear the bathroom door open. "What are you doing in there?" It's Miller!

"Taking a dump," I say.

"Finish up and come out."

I slide the magic marker down behind the toilet, but notice my hands have black all over them. I try to wipe them with a little bum wad, but no luck. So, I pull up my pants and flush the toilet. I come out with my hands in my pockets. "Hi, Mr. Miller."

"What's your name?" he demands.

"Hank."

"Hank *what*?"

"Hank Collins."

"Where's your hall pass?"

"Here," I say. I pull it out of my left pants pocket, where I'd crumpled it up.

"What's wrong with your hands?" he asks. "Hold out your hands."

I do what he says.

"Well?" he says.

"They got ink on 'em."

He looks at me for a few seconds and says, "Go back to class, Hank Collins."

I do, but about one nano-second after I sit down in class, in storms Miller, his face all purplish, and he growls from the door in a voice sounding like he's got a mouthful of sand. "Mr. Crowley, I'll be taking Hank Collins to my office."

"Fine," says Crowley.

So I shrug and roll my eyes, which makes Miller start to shake in the doorway. I got to admit I'm close to crapping my drawers, but I can't show it, so I say real slow and extended, *"What…ever!"* And then I slouch toward the door, real casual, with both hands in my pockets. By the time I get to the door, Miller looks like he's gonna explode. His left eye's got a twitch, and a big vein on his neck is sticking out about a mile. And that's not all. His left hand is opening and closing, and in his right hand he's got a wad of toilet paper that's mostly black, with the black marker tip sticking out of it.

I slide past him into the hall and turn to face him. He closes the door and takes one big step right up to me so I have to look up at him.

"You defaced the bathroom stall!" he hisses at me like some angry snake.

"No sir!" I say, real innocent and shaking my head.

"You little shit," he says. "You've been a pain in the ass all year long, and now I've got you. Your hands are black, and the marker was in the stall where you were sitting. You wrote that horrible sleaze on my walls! And don't you dare lie to me about it!"

"No sir," I say again, but this time he just can't stand it, so, with his left hand, he grabs me by the back of my neck and starts pushing me down the hall toward his office. He's going so fast, and holding me so tight, that my feet barely touch the ground. It hurts, not real bad, but bad enough for me to figure that yelling "Ow, Ouch, Ow, Ooh!" real loud can't do me any harm and might wind up being helpful. So I do.

He sits me down in the little room next to his office for what seems like years. There's nothing in there but a big rectangular table and ten hard chairs, and nothing at all for me to do, so I have plenty of time to think.

I'm in big trouble, I know that much. If I admit the thing, I'm dead meat. Maybe they'll expel me. *Probably* they'll expel me. I don't have much to lose by just sticking with the innocent routine.

Plus, I've figured out that if you lie big enough, loud enough, and long enough, it pays off. That's what the Perfect Lady said about that president she called "Slick Willy Clinton." The whole story eventually came out. Some little chick was givin' him a nob job. They even found his jizz on her dress. But he just stuck to his story, lying his ass off and insisting he'd done nothing wrong. Instead of telling the truth, he attacked the people attacking him, and just lied bigger, better, and longer. And he won! He kept his job, all his critics looked like jerks, and the American people loved him. That's the story, according to Karen, anyway.

Sue sees it different. She says that the press and some guy named Starr just wanted to get into Clinton's personal life because they hated his guts. She says that a person's sex life is his own damn business, and Clinton could do whatever he wanted with his.

But Tricky Dick was different. "Now *there* was a big time liar," she says. "He got caught and shoulda gone to jail." That's when Pete pipes up. "Yeah, but if Nixon had just burned up those tapes and had the balls to keep on lying, he would've gotten off scot-free, too."

I don't remember much about O.J. Simpson, but it sounds like he pretty much said, "That's my story and I'm sticking with it," and *he* got away with murder.

The big lie seems to win every time, so I decide to go with it. Then, in walks Miller with Sue. She's been crying, I can tell. Miller sits at the head of the table. I'm on his right, across from Sue.

He lays out the situation in a real gentle, even voice. He smiles at Sue between sentences, but he's really talking to me.

"Hank," he begins, "the truth is important, and I know your mother agrees with me when I say that we want you to do the honest and honorable thing and tell us both the truth. Do you understand?"

"Yessir," I say. I start again, "While I'm in Mr. Crowley's history class, I feel the need to go to the lavatory, so I get a hall pass and go to the bathroom. I sit down in the stall and start to do my thing, when I see this black marker on the floor. I pick it up, but it's leaking all over the place, so I get the ink all over my hands, and drop the marker back onto the floor. Then you came in." I look toward Mr. Miller as innocent and respectful as I can.

Mr. Miller shows his teeth at me again, and I wonder if he's gonna bite me, but then he nods nicely at Sue, gives one of those "ahems, ahems," into his hand, and says to me, "What else did you do in that stall?"

"After I dropped the marker, I finished up my business, and then I took some toilet paper and wrapped it around my right hand, and I leaned forward and reached down behind me to…"

"That's enough!" he almost shouts, and I can see he's trying to get a grip on, and not having much luck. "The drawings… the writing… You did that!"

"No sir," I say, shaking my head.

Now he's turning purple again and that twitch is resuming. Sue looks confused, so I can tell it's time for me to bring on the bullshit. So I put on my scaredest face and push back from the table, away from Miller, and say like I'm gonna cry, "You're not going to grab me and hurt me again, *are you*, Mr. Miller?"

Things get a little confused after that. Mr. Miller starts to shout, but Sue beats him to it. "Don't you ever touch my child!" she screams. The two of them go at it nose to nose. Words like "liar" and "litigate" and "child abuse" and "pornography" and "vandalism" and "lawyer" and "power trip" all get used.

"Don't you lay hands on my child!" says Sue.

"Your child is lying!" says Miller.

"I don't care what you say he's done, don't you touch him!"

"My actions are not the issue here. He's a vandal and…"

"You're the adult! You broke the law…"

"Are you going to let that little liar manipulate you into…"

"Don't you call my son a liar! I'll sue you for child abuse. My husband's a lawyer and…"

"Your son put pornography on my walls, and that's the only

issue here!"

The whole shouting match goes on for quite a while.

Finally, Sue grabs me by the arm and we stomp out of the school together. We're quiet all the way home, both of us staring straight ahead. When we get into the kitchen, she says to me, "Are you telling the truth?"

"Yeah," I say, and my eyes start to feel a little weepy. "He grabbed me and choked me on the way down the hall, so I started yelling. I bet some other kids even heard me. I didn't do anything wrong, but he wouldn't listen…" and then I start to really cry.

Sue gives me a big hug, and now she's crying, too. "That son-of-a-bitch is on a power trip just like every principal I ever knew. I'm calling your father to see what we're gonna do about this!"

A few minutes later, she's screaming into the phone. I can just picture Dad sitting there in his fancy office, holding the phone about a foot away from his ear. She's talking about "innocence" and "no evidence" and "child abuse" and "suing the prick and the school system for everything they have." She hangs up and says Dad's calling the principal.

About an hour later, the phone rings, and I pick it up. It's Dad. He's pretty short with me. "Put Sue on," he says. Sue takes the phone and listens for about five minutes, but I can tell she wants to interrupt by the way she's walking back and forth real fast. "He *is* telling the truth," she finally yells. "You've got to hear *his* side of it." She listens again. "Henry," she says, "why don't you hear it for yourself?" and hands me the phone.

I run the same story past Dad. I'm real convincing about the marker and seeing the pictures already there in the stall. I lay it on real thick when I get to the part about Miller grabbing me. When I finish, there's silence on the other end. Dad finally says, "Hank, are you telling me the truth?"

"Yessir," I say. There's another long silence on the other end.

Then Dad says, "Put Sue back on."

Sue listens for a long time before saying, "OK. Then you'll take care of it. Bye."

Sue hangs up, and looks over at me. "Your father says that this is a classic case of being in the wrong place at the wrong time."

"What's gonna happen?" I ask.

"Your father will take care of everything," Sue says with a big sigh.

I don't go to school the next day, which is Friday, but late in the afternoon, right after Sue gets home, Dad calls, and they talk forever.

"Here's the deal," Sue says to me after hanging up. "Your father made it clear to Mr. Miller that we won't pursue the child abuse and battery issues if Mr. Miller forgets about the graffiti. He told him that kids in class heard you screaming. He told him that you were traumatized. He also said that your story was entirely plausible, and that there was no real proof either way — that everything was circumstantial. Mr. Miller didn't like hearing that, but your father made it clear to him that he didn't have much choice. Your father has connections on the school board and is a close friend of the county solicitor. He called the solicitor, who called Miller. To make a long story short, you can go back to school on Monday."

Well, the big lie worked. Back to school I go on Monday, but living with that lie isn't as easy as I think. First, once you tell a big lie, you gotta stick with it. I might want to tell Jake the truth, but he might slip up, so now I have to lie about the whole thing to my best friend, and the big lie just gets bigger and bigger.

Then there's the Perfect Lady. She gets me alone in her kitchen about a week after the incident. She looks me straight in the face. "I'm not going to ask you what happened because I know just as well as you do. So don't waste your breath lying to me. You've fooled your father and your mother, but you haven't fooled me. You're a liar and you know it. Don't expect me to believe anything you say. Now get out of my kitchen."

Worst of all, there's Mr. Finks. One day, he asks me to stay after class. He pulls around a student desk opposite mine and, sitting directly across from me, asks me, "How are you, Hank?"

"Fine, thank you, Mr. Finks. How are *you*?"

"I'm worried about you, Hank," he says, taking off his glasses and giving them a wipe. His eyes look little and weak. "You remember Atticus Finch, don't you, Hank?"

I nod.

"Old Atticus did the right thing, didn't he? And he was a big, big man. You admired Atticus, didn't you, Hank? I seem to remember you wrote an essay on how you admired his principles."

"Yeah," I gulp. "That's right."

"It's a mighty good thing to admire a man like Atticus. Do you still admire him, Hank?"

"Yes, Mr. Finks, I do."

"Oh," he said. "Oh, Hank, I'm so glad to hear you say that. I was worried... I have to admit it. But I'm just so glad you haven't lost that feeling for what's good and true. Yes... well... ah... you've done good, Hank. Yes... and, uh, I feel better now."

I leave his room lower than a worm's belly.

So, here I sit, a coupla months later, sweating in the summer heat. After my little talk with Mr. Finks, I promised myself that I'd never lie like that again, that I didn't want to have to keep quiet about what really happened in that stall for the rest of my life.

But I know one other awful thing — the one about my Dad — and I've got to keep quiet on that one, too. If I tell the truth about that, I'll lose my family. If I say nothing, I live a lie.

I don't think I cried like that since Sue and Dad told me they were getting divorced. I sat where the frogs lived, near my river, with my bike. But I felt more alone than I've ever felt before.

Chapter 9

Still feeling pretty low, I slowly leave my pond-thinking log, get onto my bike, and start cycling back up the trail towards home. I watch only the ground right in front of me, and only for rocks and logs, so I don't see much until I'm right on top of it. Your world on a bike is pretty small — just the stuff that rolls by you moment by moment. That's why I practically run over this guy before I even see him.

He's backing out onto the bike trail from a laurel bush, and I look up just in time to hit the brakes and to get mooned. Right in front of me, I see half of a big old white butt over low-rise camouflage cargo pants. Perfect Lady calls the droopy-drawered, crack-above-the-belt-look "plumber's backside," and I practically run smack dab into it here in the woods. Who woulda predicted that?

The guy's stooped over, hunch-back like, and turns his round soft body real slow to face me. He's blubbering, with tears streaming down his face, which looks and sounds silly 'cause he's got G.I. Joe green-and-black face-paint on. Goggles are up on top of his army cap. He stands there in the middle of the path, blocking me and weeping. His hands are down at his crotch.

"What's wrong, man?" I ask.

"Nothin'," the guy says.

"OK, then," I say, "get outta the path."

I start to push past him, but he says, "Please, no, don't go. I need help. I need your help."

So I stop and look at him for a second. I can't see anything wrong, except he's standing all round-shouldered and real still, and his hands are still on his crotch. "What kinda help do you need?" I ask.

He lets out a long sigh-sob. "While I was playing paintball, I had to take a leak. I hid real careful, and knew I hadda be fast. I didn't get all the way up. I just knelt, keeping my eyes open for the enemy. I kept my gun in my right hand and did my thing left-handed, which is not my usual way. Then I couldn't get my fly up one-handed. So I gave my fly a real hard jerk and now I've got my foreskin caught in my zipper. I can't stand up straight. I can barely breathe. And, man, does it hurt…"

The guy's a real mess, and I'm feeling sorry for him now 'cause he's so pathetic. "What can *I* do?" I ask.

"I don't know, I don't know," he squeaks. "I can't seem to fix it."

This situation is way past weird, but he's the sorriest looking guy I've ever seen. I can't just leave him there, I guess, but I hesitate. Finally, I say, "Do you want me to take a look?"

"Would you?" he looks at me red-eyed. "I can't see it real well. I can't tell how exactly it's caught."

So I get off my bike and bend over in front of him. This is just too weird, I'm thinking to myself. But I see his fly is about three quarters up. About an inch below the top, I can see this flap of skin sticking out. "Well," I say to him, "there's only one thing to do, and that's to pull your fly down. You just gotta pull your fly down."

"I can't. It'll hurt too much."

"It's caught pretty good," I say. "If you try yanking it out, you'll probably rip part of it off."

"Oh shit, oh shit," he says, shaking all over and sniffling.

"What're you going to do, man?"

The guy's silent for a few seconds, looking at his feet. Then he looks at me, sadly, and asks, "Can *you* pull my fly down?"

"Shit, no!" I say, taking a step backwards. "I'm not touching you, man." I'm starting to think this man is a pervert or something.

But then he starts crying again and saying, "What am I going to do? What am I going to do?"

We just stare at each other for what seems like a lifetime. Am I gonna leave this sniveling plumber-butt alone in the woods with his tears smudging his camouflage and his foreskin in his zipper? "OK," I say.

"*OK?*" he asks, not sure I'd given him a "yes."

"OK," I say again. "Grab ahold of the top of your pants real tight with both hands."

He does, but he yelps real hard like a hurt puppy 'cause it tightens the fly. Then I grab the top of his zipper and yank down as hard and fast as I can. He gives out a short bark. Then there's silence, the two of us just standing there, facing each other, and saying nothing.

Finally, he takes a real deep breath. "Thanks, man," he says. Then he turns his back to me, starts fumbling around his crotch, and looks down.

"The tip… " he starts to say, but I interrupt him.

"That's OK, man, I don't need to know…"

"No," he says, "it's OK. The tip's just a little bloody. No big deal."

He gives me a big grin, showing off these brownish, stained teeth, and puts out his right hand to give me a shake, when, "FWOP!"

He takes a hit right in the forehead and falls backwards. I dive into the bushes, scared shitless, and lie with my head down. Then there's this big laugh from about ten yards down the trail.

"I got you, Fred, you sorry-ass sumbitch. Stand up in combat and you pay the price."

I peek around the edge of a sycamore trunk and see this huge black-haired, bearded guy, also in camo, striding up the path. He's holding a paintball gun and laughing.

This was my introduction to "Fred the zipper guy" and his paintball arch-enemy Top.

Fred is sitting in the middle of the trail, legs splayed apart, looking almost as ridiculous as my first view of him. He's wiping his face with his sleeve while red paint oozes through his eyebrows and drips onto his cheeks. Top got Fred square between the eyes.

"Who are *you?*" asks Top as I come out of the bushes.

"Hank."

Fred starts grunting up to his feet, saying, "Top, Hank here helped me out. He's a good kid." Then, talking a million miles an hour, he blurts out the whole ridiculous story. Top starts to laugh and looks at me.

"My friends call me Top, and you've already met Fred, the fuck-up. Nice to meet you, Hank." He holds out a hand that's at the end of a huge hairy forearm. We shake hands and he just about breaks mine.

Top proceeds to tell me that sergeants in 'Nam were called Top. "My men call me Top, my friends call me Top, and there's no question, I like to be on top, if you know what I mean," he says, giving me a big, knowing wink.

Fred wants to shake hands with me, too. We do, and Fred wants to know if I like paintball. When he hears I've never played, he tells me what I'm missing and talks about crawling around in the woods, running all over the place, and shooting each other.

I find myself liking "Fred the fuck-up" even though he spits when he talks. There's something nice about the way he gets all excited and jumbles up his words. "D'ya wanna play?" he asks, his rush of words ending with a sudden, breathless stop.

"Now, hold on there," Top interrupts before I can answer. "Hank here might not be right for this game. It's serious stuff, and requires some training. We can't let just anybody into the Gunpowder Paintball Squad. He'll have to show us what he can do."

Paintball sounds like fun, but I act like I don't care about it one way or the other. Also, I never saw these two dudes before, and they seem a little old to be running around in the woods shooting each other.

Fred asks, "What does he have to do?"

Top scratches his dark bristly chin like he's thinking. "H-m-m-m," he says slowly. Then he squats in the path and picks up a dry twig, which he fiddles with for a while. Then, standing up, he tosses the twig away like he's reached a carefully considered conclusion of great importance.

"We'll give you a tryout at the electronic warfare school. If you do good, I'll make you a member of our squad. If you stink the place up, you're out. That's my final word on the matter."

"OK?" Fred asks me, nodding and smiling. "Will you do it? We'll have fun. I bet you'll be good."

Just looking at him with the red paint on top of his green and black-streaked face, his brownish teeth looking almost bright in a big goofy grin, I have to smile back. I wanna do it, but I'm still hesitating. "Can I bring a friend?" I ask.

"Sure," says Top.

"OK, then!" Fred practically shouts. "We'll have a tryout."

I'm not sure I ever really said "yes," but we make arrangements to meet next week and then drive together to the testing site.

I figure I can just show up if I want to, and stay home if I decide against it.

Chapter 10

Jake can't come with me to the paintball tryout because of baseball, so I nearly chicken out, but I've been looking forward to this war game stuff all week because it seems way cool. Besides, I got zero to do with my time, and this summer is turning out to be a major zero. I gotta find something to do to keep me sane.

The days have just dragged by, and it's been ugly, burn-your-ass-on-the-car-seat hot. Muggy, too, so you start sweating just thinking about doing something. My face becomes a grease factory on weeks like this, and I grow these mountains of zits on my back. I can bend over the sink, reach around, and give a ripe one a hard pinch. If it explodes just right, I can hit the mirror.

Also, everything seems kind of rotten when the weather gets like this. Grass clumps go under the mower, and when you scrape it out, has a real sick-sweet smell to it. The roads steam after an afternoon shower, and the tar/rubber smell almost sticks to the roof of your mouth. The cows look miserable in the fields, standing there dumb with the flies buzzing all around them, and the only thing that stinks worse than them are the hogs. They wallow in their muddy pens and their own crap. It's enough to make you a vegetarian.

Anyhow, we're supposed to meet in the WaWa parking lot near the Mt. Carmel exit for Hereford, and neither of my families knows anything about it. The Perfect Lady believes I'm at Sue's, and Sue thinks I'm with the Perfect Lady. Since they don't talk much, it's pretty easy to pull this scam off.

So I lock my bike up out of sight behind the store and am waiting on the curb when Top's big red Chevy truck comes rolling in. There's goofy Fred waving at me through the passenger window like a four-year-old kid. He jumps out of the truck cab like a sloppy old St. Bernard, yanks up his droopy drawers, which look like they might fall down to his ankles at any moment, and hollers, "Hiya, Hank!"

Top gets out the other side. A cigarette sits on his lower lip as he strolls around the truck bed. "Ready to go, boy?" he asks.

I nod. "Gotta get me some Joe first," says Top. He's wearing a black baseball cap that says "Follow Me" in yellow letters on the front. His t-shirt's olive drab, and I can see on his right bicep a blue tattoo, old and faded looking, but I can make out the words "duty, honor, country." There's an eagle's head, too.

We go into the WaWa and I roam around a little, buy a pack of gum, and head back outside. Top comes out with Fred and we all get in the truck. I'm in the back seat, so I'm staring at the back of their heads. The back window has this eagle on it. It says 101st Airborne. There's a little Confederate flag decal on the back window, too. And up above is a gun rack.

Top starts the motor up and takes a sip of his coffee. He looks over at Fred for a second. "Well?" he asks, as if Fred knows exactly what he means.

"*What?*" Fred replies in this little voice.

"What'd you swipe this time, Fatso?"

"Oh, nothin' much, just these Tic Tacs from next to the register."

Top turns toward me a little. "Fred's a klepto," he says with a grunt.

"Yup, I'm a klepto," Fred agrees happily. "Can't help it. Always takin' somethin' with me as a souvenir. Just little stuff though. Nothin' big."

We back out and then pull onto Mt. Carmel Road. A hundred yards down, we take a left onto I-83 South. I like 83. It's a river of cars, and its flow changes depending on the time of day and the weather. I also like the place where the Gunpowder slides under 83. You can stand in the water there, in the shade of the bridges, and almost get chilled on a July evening.

Swallows live there — under the bridge, I mean — and they swoop down off the water to eat bugs and stuff. It's quiet except for the hollow zoom-zump-thump the cars make as they roll over the bridge seams. The car travelers above don't even know I'm down there underneath them. They might never even know a river of fish and swallows and tubers is slipping under their tires. They're just heading somewhere — serious men and women in business clothes going to work. Families on vacation. Couples having fights. Drunks. Dogs hanging their heads out the side windows. Kids listening to head-banging music and doing a joint. They're all traveling overtop my river, going north and going south, real fast, in their private little car worlds, clueless that I'm even there. I like that, though it's a lonely feeling if you stay there and listen too long

Now I'm with "Fat Fred the Klepto Man," grinning at me from the front seat while Top drinks his coffee and stares out the windshield. We're a pretty weirded-out trio if you ask me, goin' along 83, probably passing right over some kid in the river below. Top says, "We're headed toward Dundalk and the Golden Ring Mall. The warfare training school's right in there, and we'll see what you're made of."

"OK," I say and then ask, "Top, where'd you go in the Army?"

"All over the stinkin' world," he says, and then off he goes. "Spent twenty years, lifer, took retirement at 38. Finished up at Ft. Campbell, Kentucky, hell of a shit hole — 101st Airborne, screaming eagles, Battle of the Bulge in WW2, and all that shit. We were good in 'Nam, boy, damn good. Saw action damn near every fucking place. Khe Son, Quanng Tri, Mekong Delta. I was 11 Bravo, Infantry soldier, sergeant, E-6 going in and an E-8, first sergeant, coming home. I was there for Tet. Shit, what a mess! We kicked the piss outta those little gooks, didn't lose once, but the papers back home made it sound like we were losing.

"It was FUBAR, man — Fucked Up Beyond All Recognition. The Cong would kiss your ass by day and sneak around in their black pajamas at night, fraggin' your ass. Same people. Smilin' and noddin' to start, and then blowin' up some ammo dump to finish. Sneaky little bastards…"

He goes on and on while we drive around the Beltway. After awhile, I just tune most of it out. Then Fred turns around and says loud and excited, "Make him learn the marching songs, Top. Sing out the way you did cadence when you marched around the base."

"OK, men," Top says, "sound off after me!"

Then he half shouts-half sings, and we repeat the words after every line. It's weird and cool at the same time.

> *I wanna be an airborne ranger!*
> *I wanna live a life of danger!*
> *I wanna kill some Viet Cong!*
> *Hail, Hail, Captain Jack!*
> *Meet me down the railroad track!*
> *I got a nickel bag in my hand!*

I wanna be a smoking man!
Hail, Hail, Army!
Hail, Hail, Infantry!
We're the best, it's plain to see!
Airborne, ranger infantry!

Over and over we do them — all kinds of marching songs, and all at the top of our lungs. Fred is joyfully spitting out the words all over the inside of the front windshield. Top's voice just seems to get louder and louder. When we pull off the exit ramp and stop at a light, people in the car next to us stare. One little girl has her face up against the glass of the back window, unable to take her eyes off us. To her, we're three far-out dudes, which is just fine with me.

We get out of the truck, and the mall looks real familiar to me, like I've been here before. We go in and head toward the "Ultrazone," which I know because I've been coming here to birthday parties since I was about ten. I love the place. You get a little vest and a gun, and you play team laser-tag for hours. You run around in the dark and act sneaky. Then, afterwards, you get a team score and an individual score. I was always major good. Me and Jake won like every time we were on a team together.

Suddenly, it dawns on me. *This* is what Top has been calling the Warfare Training School. *What a joke!*

"This is the Ultrazone, where little kids come to play!" I say to Top.

He stops walking and looks at me for a second. "Maybe we were wrong about you, Private. Maybe you're just one of those sniveling pukes who can't get the big picture. Sure, little kids run around in there, but if you know what you're doing, it's a great way to evaluate combat talent. Now, if you can't see that, maybe you just don't have what it takes. What's it gonna be?"

I have trouble looking him in the eye while he's staring me down, so I look down at my feet. We had fun in the truck and I don't wanna screw up the day, but this whole thing strikes me as more than a bit bogus. Warfare training school it ain't. But what the hell? Maybe it'll be fun.

Fred says, "You'll see, Hank. It's great. You'll like it. Come on!"

"OK," I say, looking at Top. "I'll take it serious."

"Good," he says, "then let's get moving."

The first game is a riot. The three of us are put up against five ten-year-olds, who are there with a mom. The combat area is dark and has stairs and walls and passageways. You get ten minutes to shoot as much as you can, while you try to keep from getting shot. Your vest lights up when they hit you, and theirs light up when you hit them. I'm an absolute maniac shooting these little kids.

I see Fred, though. He's always out of breath and some little kid is forever nailing him. Top is always standing in some corner shooting kids as they go past, but he's an easy target and doesn't seem to notice he's always lit up like a Christmas tree.

We get out and get our scores. Man, did those little kids ever smoke us! They had triple our score! Fred got shot over one hundred times, and Top wasn't too far behind him. I only got shot twelve times, but I shot about 200. Fred, who shot 10, says his gun was "jammed," whatever that means. Top shot 48. We sucked big time, but I was the high scorer for the game from either side and won a free Coke.

"We gotta post-mortem this fucker!" Top says, so we sit down and talk strategy. "Just like the gooks, they got the advantage 'cause they're little and sneaky. We're big and obvious. The game puts more demands on us, makes it a bigger challenge for us, so we got to adapt to the environment, and go native. You keep moving, Hank, 'cause you're almost one of them in size. You can work behind lines, infiltrate those bastards, and blow 'em away. Fred, you'll be our distraction since you're a fat-fuck and can't move anyway. You stay in one area and make noise. Try to get them to come to you. I'll slide around in covert ops nearby and shoot the little monkeys as they come towards you. They'll be scared by Hank runnin' around behind lines, so they'll want to come to Fred, the big bleating cow, 'cause it's easy. That's where I'll be, slitting throats as they come to Momma!"

In we go again for the second time. This time it's three teenagers we're up against. They're into the Goth look, dressed all in black, with black hair and pierced everything, but they seem really into the game. We try to do what Top says, and Fred does make a pretty good target. They shoot him a bunch of times. When the whole thing is over, we get our scores, and boy, we sucked even worse. Top tells us why.

"We prepared for the Cong but got the regular North Vietnamese Army. Regulars fight different than sneak-and-peekers. They're good in an open firefight 'cause they have discipline. Our tactics were all wrong for this group and we failed to adjust. Lesson learned. Gotta change on the fly."

It sounds close to total bullshit to me, but I still have a great time. Top and Fred are totally into it even if they do suck. My score is high again, so I win another Coke, which I share with Fred, who now has big sweat stains under his armpits and is panting like a dog.

Top says he's learned enough about how I work, and that I'll be a "good addition" to the Gunpowder Paintball Squad because my style "contrasts and complements" theirs. This makes Fred hop around from foot to foot in a little congratulatory dance, singing "Hoo-Hah, Yeah-Yeah."

After Fred's done, Top continues, "Small arms units are best with a variety of skills — makes 'em more dangerous." Then he asks if I've got the dough to buy myself a paintball gun and some protective goggles. I say, yeah, probably, depending on how much they cost, and he says that's cool and asks if maybe I'd be interested in going with him and Fred to a big-time paintball war later in August up in Pennsylvania somewhere — that is, of course, if I turn out to be good in the woods during "maneuvers" near the Gunpowder.

I shrug and say, "Whatever," but inside I'm thinking, "This is going to be totally cool." Top says the tournament in Pennsylvania lasts three days, with two nights of sleeping-over in tents. You drive up on a Friday and drive home Sunday evening. I like campfires and sleeping in tents and shit like that, so the whole deal sounds great to me.

On the way back to Hereford in the truck, we learn how to sound off the right way. Top shouts sing-song and we answer:

> *You ain't got no friends on your left!*
> *You're right!*
> *You ain't got no friends on your right!*
> *You're left.*
> *Sound off.*
> *One, two!*
> *Sound off!*
> *Three, four!*
> *One, two, three, four!*
> *One, two!*
> *Three, four!*

It's fun singing back and forth. When I get back home, Jake's hanging out, so I tell him all about it. He gets excited about the paintball idea, too, but he says no way about the Pennsylvania trip 'cause, as he puts it, if Karen caught him trying to tag along, she'd end his life "in a sudden and horrid manner." We decide, though, to buy paintball guns and ammo for both of us, and wonder whether Dick's Sporting Goods stocks that stuff down at Hunt Valley Mall.

Chapter 11

At Dick's, Jake and me buy paintball guns and a bunch of ammo. We get goggles and camo hats, too. We practice all week and on Saturday meet up with Top and Fred at the WaWa.

When we go into the store, Jake gets a Coke. I don't feel like much, so I just follow Fred around to see if he'll do his klepto thing. I don't see him lift a thing. Top gets his usual coffee and out to the truck we go, with me and Jake in the back.

Top looks at Fred, "Well?" he asks.

"*What?*"

"What you get this time?"

Fred smiles his little kid smile. "Just some gum. Hank likes gum, so I got some gum. Want some?" he asks Top.

Boy, he's one good klepto, I think to myself.

"No," says Top and he starts to back out of the space, twisting around to look between me and Jake. He gives Jake a wink. "You any good, boy?"

Before Jake can say anything, I answer for him. "Better than me."

"We'll see," says Top.

We drive over to the Loch Raven Reservoir, down a pretty crummy old road, and park in an area that says, "No parking."

Top sets all the rules. "Hank and Jake against Top and Fred," he says. So we go into the woods and sit for the specified five minutes. Then we start to sneak around inside the boundary area Top has set.

Jake and me stay within sight of each other and we find Fred crouched down behind an oak, with his back to us. Jake shoots him right in the butt, and Fred yelps like a dog whose tail's been stepped on.

"Shit," he says, "you just about scared me crazy."

"You're out!" Jake whispers, but almost the second he says it, he gets clobbered on the side of the head just above the temple. It knocks him over, and sprays paint all over his hair and face. "Ouch!" he yells. "That hurt like hell."

I hear Top laugh but can't see him. His laugh comes from across the little out-of-bounds path. I start to yell, "You're out of bounds…" but before I finish, I catch one full in the chest. There's paint all over my t-shirt, and boy, those things do sting like hell.

Top comes striding out from behind a tree and laughing. "I got you sniveling pukes while you were gloating over your kill. After you waste the enemy is when you're most vulnerable. You gotta shoot and move right away, shoot and sink right back into cover."

"You cheated!" Jake protests.

Top looks at him, "All's fair in love and war!"

It kinda pisses me off to lose like that, and Jake is sullen about it as we walk back to the pick-up. But I gotta admit it — Top's a good shot, and we shouldn't have been standing around like that. Back at the truck, we drink water from Army canteens and sit in the grass talking.

Top tells us about a firefight at Quangtri, where he and a squad from his platoon are pinned down at night. He calls in some mortar support, but they screw up the coordinates and drop the rounds right on top of him and his boys, and he catches some shrapnel in the calf. To show us the old scar, which is about the size of a stick of gum and all purplish, he rolls up his fatigue pant leg.

"One of my men is gut-shot and starts screamin', so I grab him by the top of his web gear and start haulin' him out of there. We get to a designated landing zone, and try to call in some choppers, but there's not a Huey anywhere in sight. We just crouch there in the bushes. Finally the choppers show and we get evacced out. I got the Bronze Star, a Purple Heart, and a month of R and R in Saigon — not bad, huh?"

We sit quietly for awhile. Fred's pickin' his nose with a dandelion stem. You can hear the buzzing sound from all the insects. It's good to be in the shade because the day's starting to do its furnace thing. Jake looks at Top and asks, "So what'd you do after you got out?"

"I got a job as a mail carrier," says Top, "but I hurt my back about three years ago — a disk problem — so I can't lift nothing. I'm on disability. Every six months I go in and they see if the bulge in the disc is still there. It's not goin' anywhere. Not bad work if you can get it — my Army retirement check and my Post Office check come in every month like clockwork. Uncle Sam takes care of his own, but you gotta know how to work the system, too."

"How old are you, Top?" I ask him.

He pauses a moment. "Just a few months short of my fiftieth birthday, and here I am hangin' out with you three snivelin' pukes. Holy shit!" He takes a long drink from his canteen. "I don't know how, but this life just sneaks past you without much warnin'. Seems like yesterday when I was just seventeen years old and gettin' out of Havre de Grace High School."

"That where you from?" I ask.

"Yup, lived there until the draft got me. Then it was the Army. Me and Fred live over in Sparks now."

Fred nodded. "Sparks is a nice place to live. I like being near the river. It's easy to get to Hunt Valley for the movies, and there's plenty of good food places on York Road. You ever try that barbecue by the fair grounds in Timonium? M-m-m-m! I drool just thinkin' about those ribs…"

"What do you do?" Jake interrupts. "What kinda work are you in?" he asks Fred.

"Plumber's helper."

Top laughs. "Yeah, he's been an assistant for ten years now, so I don't think he's movin' up in the world real fast."

"I like it," Fred says eagerly. "I hand the right tools for the job to the plumber and help him hold stuff and keep stuff straight. I tighten stuff up, too, and unclog drains with the snake. Sometimes I do digging outside. We get to go into lots of nice houses and talk to nice people. They always tell us how glad they are to see us come. Then they thank us lots when we fix their problem. It's a very nice kind of job to have, and the plumber is a nice man. I like it the way it is. Nice…"

Fred just runs outta steam after his little speech — the words all sorta fall out of his mouth on top of each other. He barely breathes.

We're all quiet for a moment. Jake's smirking at Fred. I'm thinking, "It's hard not to like the silly sucker."

"And where are you from, Fred?" Jake asks him.

"Bel Air."

"Your folks still live there?"

"I guess so. Haven't seen them in twenty-two years."

"How old are you? You don't look all that old."

"I'm thirty-six."

"Hold it," says Jake, who I can see is doing some quick figuring. "You haven't seen your folks since you were fourteen? That can't be right."

Fred just sits there sadly and doesn't answer.

Top butts in, "They threw him outta the house when he was thirteen-years-old. Guess he was too much of a klepto for them."

"No, *really*?" I ask, but Fred just nods.

"They never let you come home again?" I say. "That makes no sense."

"You think the world makes sense," Top says, real sarcastic. "You livin' on another planet, boy? You want sense, go cash a dollar bill. That's the only cents you can count on."

Jake is watching Fred real intense. "So what'd you do?" he asks him.

When he starts to answer, Fred seems to be coming back from some dream, and he talks real slow and deliberate. "First, I tried stayin' at friends' houses and just goin' to school on the bus, but I only had three or four friends I could do that with, and that got old after a month. Then I found I could sleep in unlocked cars in the neighborhood and share people's lunches at school.

"One morning, a guy drove almost all the way to work without noticing me asleep in the backseat. When I sat up, he damn near drove underneath a semi. He was yelling, 'Jesus, Joseph, and Mary! What're you doing back there, you little cocksucker?!' I'll never forget it. He put me out, right there on the Beltway, so I'm sittin' on the guard rail, cryin' and watchin' the cars go flying by. Finally, a cop comes up, and asks me stuff, but I'm scared and can barely even remember my name. So then it all started."

"What?" I ask.

"Shelters, foster homes, runnin' away and being brought back
… juvenile detention for stealing food and stuff from stores."

"How long did that last?'

"'Till I turned eighteen."

"And then what?"

"I tried to join the Army, but I've got a heart murmur, and I'm
fat, and my teeth are rotten, and I don't breathe good, especially when
it's cold out, so they don't take me. I got a job as a laborer. It was nice.
I would dig and pile stuff up and do whatever needed being done, and
I got an apartment for myself and my own TV. Then I got laid off and
went on unemployment, but since I was a good worker and always
showed up on time, I got a call after about six months and went back
to work. I met the plumber about a year later, and he liked my hard
work, and took me on. I'll never get laid off, the plumber said, and
that's 'cause there's one absolute truth to life. He says you got to shit
to live, and I think he's right, so I'm stayin' with him. I got security
with him, and, as far as I'm concerned, that's the most important
thing."

"Yeah, but you steal stuff," I say.

Fred frowns. "Not from the plumber, and not from people's
houses — just little stuff from stores and from mean people. They
don't miss it. I can't help it, anyway. It's like I'm watchin' myself do it,
which is kind of a weird feeling. I know it's gonna happen, and then
it does, sorta all by itself."

"You got some real assholes for parents," Jake says. "Don't you
kinda wonder how they're doing?"

"Nope," Fred says angry and hard. "Nope, nope, nope. When
my dad threw me out, he said, 'You're dead to me.' Mom just stood
there cryin'. So now they're dead *to me*, and I don't go to Bel Air for

nothin'."

"Nuff said," Top interrupts. "Let's go another round in the bush. Same teams. Learn from your mistakes. Kick some butt!"

Now that Jake and I know the rules, we're all ready for more action.

Chapter 12

After going cold for a while, Jake's baseball team has now been hot for three straight weeks, driving in a mess of runs and winning every game. Coach moved Jake from second to short, where he's doing good, but still doesn't move early enough on the crack of the bat, if you listen to him. But Jake's harder on himself than anyone else is. And, believe it or not, Coach still makes the team run sprints after every practice. What an A-hole!

You can't quarrel with the results, though. Jake's team is playing in the regional quarter-finals tonight, and I'll be proud to watch from the stands. It's the first time I've seen the team play since I quit. The crowd — maybe a hundred people — is pretty good sized, at least for a Little League game on a hot July night. A group of old people have pulled up lawn chairs in deep, deep right center, way past where any of the kids can hit it, but where an old oak tree offers some shade and cooler temperatures. They still sit there fanning themselves — about a dozen of 'em.

Along the first base line, before you get to the hot dog stand, sit a bunch of girls I know from school, and a bunch I don't know. They hold onto the chain link fence, giggling, squealing, and generally acting like they're nuts. They're in summer uniform — real little denim shorts that ride up the cracks of their asses so they're always tugging at their butts — and little tube-tops and halter-tops. If they've got big boobs, they pull their tank-tops real low and extra tight.

They all wear their hair up off their necks in a ponytail or in that thing the Perfect Lady calls a "French braid." Most of 'em look pretty good, I've got to admit. I walk over to get a dog, and act as if I don't see the girls, but a few of them turn and look at me. "Hey," I say. A girl named Marcie, who was in English class with me and who I've talked to a bunch of times, says, "Hey, Hank. How's it goin'? And why aren't *you* playin'?"

She's about five-foot-two, with real dark hair and a full rack that seems to be standing at attention and looking straight at me. I try real hard to look just at her face, and not to stare at her chest, but those babies are like eye magnets, so I give up and just sort of look at the ground. When I see girls, I wish I'd notice something else besides boobs and ass, but that's what I see. It's not even voluntary.

"Hey, Marcie. I quit the team about a month ago — couldn't stand the coach — but I'm doin' good, just sorta hangin' out. What're you up to?"

"I'm checkin' out groceries at a food store. BO-ring! But I go down to the shore some weekends with Mom and my sisters." I bet Marcie looks real hot in a two-piece.

When Jake's team takes the field, everybody in the wooden bleachers starts to clap. The girls at the fence scream and jump up and down.

"All the girls think Jake's hot," Marcie says, "especially Ginny. She says she'd, like, die for him."

I'm thinking to myself, "Ginny's got an older look, and a major rep for goin' all the way with the high school guys. But who knows what's true?" I look over and spot Ginny, standing at the fence, just as she screams out, "Go Jake!" She's got blond hair and is almost as tall as Jake. Long legs. Real tight body. Built like a jock.

Jake's cool. He never looks or pays any attention, but he hears. I can tell.

"She really said that?" I ask Marcie.

"Yup!" she says.

"What's she mean by that?"

"Duh," says Marcie, giving me one of those dumb faces, with her head cocked and her hip pushed out to the side. "What do *you* think? She wants to study algebra with him? I *don't* think so."

"I wanna get a hot dog. You want somethin'?"

"Sure," Marcie says.

We walk past the girls and they all start to giggle. I can tell they're watchin' us as we walk toward the concession stand. The giggling gets real loud, and I even hear my name mentioned. I hate that shit. I get so self-conscious that I can barely breathe.

Marcie gets a Diet Coke. I get two dogs with ketchup and a Coke. We go to the end of the bleachers and then all the way up to the top row. I can see the Perfect Lady and Stephie in about row two at the other end. Stephie is yelling out Jake's name about every ten seconds. Marcie asks me why she hasn't seen me around at all this summer.

"I dunno," I say. "I've been messin' around with my bike and hanging around down at the Gunpowder, and I've been playing paintball with some older guys I met," but I don't tell her how old they actually are.

"You've missed some good parties," she says. "The high school kids scope out somebody's house after the parents go outta town. I hear there's going to be a big party this weekend over in Monkton. Why don't you and Jake come?"

I don't want to tell her — Sue would let me go, but the Perfect

Lady would go completely berserk if Jake or me even asked about going to a party like that.

"Sounds good," I say.

"Ginny will be there, and I'm tellin' you, she's hot for Jake, and we all could hang out together if you wanted."

I look for the first time at Marcie's face — up from my feet, that is — and she's smiling at me. All of a sudden, I can feel myself getting stupid. My eyes travel down to her chest, and I just say, "I'd like that," like the complete dork that I am.

She says, "Good," and she puts her hand on my hand, which freaks me out almost completely. I try to stay cool, and just kinda turn my hand over, until we're holding hands. I have no clue how to act at this point, so I just watch the baseball game. I've got absolutely nothing to say, but Marcie more than makes up for it. I think she musta talked for about four innings without drawing a breath.

She talks about what a pain in the ass her boss is, how the girl at the next register steals stuff, how the bagger at her station squishes fruit on purpose, how the kids all hang out after work and smoke cigarettes, which she thinks is totally gross, how she went shopping for a new bathing suit with her sister, Tina, who is sixteen, how she got a totally hot suit that makes her look older, which is good, how Tina is "doing it" with her boyfriend, how her sister got a diaphragm 'cause she's "scared of the pill and cancer," how they decided to "do it" 'cause they were just giving each other hand jobs and having oral sex, and that just wasn't "doing it" for them.

She goes on and on, telling me stuff that's totally none of my business, and even though I'm not interested in the stuff she's telling me, except about her sister, I do like hearing her talk, all enthusiastic, and then when she finally does pause during the top of the fifth inning, she says, "You know, Hank, you're a really good listener."

Like the dork I am, I can think of nothin' smart to say back to her, so, as usual, I just say, "Thanks." I think there's a big difference between being a good listener and just sitting there like a box of rocks, not having a clue what to say. But if she can't tell the difference, maybe just sitting there dumb is a pretty good way to go. Maybe I'll work on lookin' smart when I'm listening. That might work — unless she asks me questions, 'cause all I can ever think of to say is, "Yup" or "Nope," and that pretty much is a showstopper unless she's got more to say.

In the fifth, Jake makes a great play moving to his right and throwing across his body to just get the third out at first. I yell, "Way to go, Jake," and let go of Marcie's hand to stand and clap as he comes off the field. The problem is, when I sit down again, I can't figure how to get hold of her hand again without seeming to be totally bogus. So I just make my hand available and Marcie reaches over and grabs it, which solves my dorkiness for me.

We're pretty quiet after that, so I decide that, if I ask Marcie a question, maybe that'll get her talkin' again. So I ask her, "What movies you seen lately?" And she's off! That gets us to the bottom of the seventh, when Jake comes to bat with one out and the winning run on first. Marcie, who must see I've stopped listening, says to me, "Jake's up."

Being the conversational genius that I am, I say, "Yup."

The runner leaves first on the pitch, and Jake slaps the ball perfectly to the right side, behind the runner and the second baseman, who's gone to second to cover on the steal. The right fielder charges the ball, but his throw to third is late. "Great baseball, man!" I jump up and yell. "Way to go, Jake!" He's smiling standing there on first, and the girls along the fence are jumping all around and squealing. On the first pitch, Jake breaks for second, and the catcher actually tries to throw him out on the steal. Jeez, man, what is that stupid catcher thinking?! His dumb, dorky play lets the man on third practically walk home for the winning run. I can see their coach is gonna burst a vein or something, but it's too late. The game is over.

I'm standin' there, and Marcie is standin' there next to me, when she reaches around my waist with her arm. My arm is kinda stuck, awkward, in front of her, but I gotta do something or I'll win the "Geek of the Year" award. I bring my own arm over her head and she ducks to keep me from knockin' her clear off the back of the bleachers. Good thing she's quick! Now my arm's around her and we're just standing there and I have absolutely no clue whatsoever what to do next.

Then Marcie says, "Let's go down and see Jake," and she starts down the bleachers having managed, with no sweat, to get her arm out from around me and my hand in hers. I wonder if girls are just born knowing how to do this stuff. I wonder if boys are all total dorks like me. Jake always looks cool and relaxed, but I'll have to remember to ask him anyway what he thinks.

I follow Marcie down to the area just inside the fence on the first base side, where the players and the girls have all started to mix. I see that Ginny is right next to Jake, and she's grabbed his hat and is wearing it sideways. Jake, as usual, looks cool and mellow. He's laughing at Ginny, and tells her to give him back the cap. She doesn't. He makes a grab for it, and she ducks and walks away. Now he's wrestling around with her and she's laughing. So's he. He's not trying too hard to get the hat, and she's not trying too hard to get away.

While all this is going on, I've got my arm around Marcie again, but I have no clue how that happened. She's talking and laughing. As

I'm looking around, I spot the Perfect Lady in the stands. She's watching all of us with kind of a funny expression on her face. "Uh-oh," I think to myself. That's when Stephie pops up beside me and says, "Jake's the hero, right, Hank?"

"Yup, Stephie," I say. "Jake's the hero!" She goes skipping straight over to Jake and gives his leg a big hug before he even sees her.

"You're the hero, Jake!"

"Thanks, Steph," Jake says, and puts his hand on her head real gentle before brushing some hair out of her face. "Thanks."

"Let's go home, Jake. I'm hungry," Stephie tells him.

"Me, too!" Jake says.

He says goodbye to Ginny, but I don't know how to get untangled from Marcie, so I just say, "Gotta go."

She looks up at me and says, "I know, but you'll see me at the party, right? My sister can take us."

I don't know what to say, so I just stand there and again say, "Gotta go."

"I'll call you," she says.

"OK," I say, and having wrapped up "Nerd of the Decade" honors with an award-winning performance, I follow Jake and Stephie to the parking lot.

Before unlocking the van, the Perfect Lady gives Jake a big hug. "Way to go, champ," she says. I can see he's happy. He gets in the front, and I get in the back with Stephie. Jake gives us all the game details and the cool stuff going on in the dugout. He turns and looks at me. "Can you believe that catcher threw to second with one out and a man on third?" he says. "What was he thinking? And then he could only get it to second on about three hops, so the whole thing was a joke. I bet he's catching hell from everybody."

At home, we get into the kitchen, where I shuck corn while Jake cleans up. Then he slices the tomatoes, and Stephie sets the table. The Perfect Lady has a tuna fish casserole that she's been cooking on low the whole time we were out, and now it's ready. The corn will be cooked before we finish a first helping of the tuna.

After the Perfect Lady says grace, we all eat, and it's quiet for a few moments, but, from my memory of the expression on Karen's face up in the bleachers after the game, I know there's a question she's just itchin' to ask.

"Jake," the predictably perfect woman says real innocent and casual, which is when she's most dangerous 'cause you can't tell for sure which way she's goin', "who was the young lady paying you so much attention after the game?"

"Which one?" Jake asks, which is the perfect answer 'cause it drives her crazy and makes her give out the details that show she was spying on him.

She stays with it, though. "Long blond hair, tall and thin." She didn't add tight little butt, but I know what she's thinkin': "Ginny's a little tart who's goin' after my boy."

Jake looks up and says with a mouthful, "Geez, Mom, there were like dozens of blond girls there. How'm I supposed to know?"

He manages to hit her buttons perfectly, and she blurts out, "Don't speak with your mouth full, Jake, and don't be thick. You know perfectly well who I'm talkin' about — that girl with the short-shorts who took your cap, that one who you were wrestling around with."

"Oh, her," he says with his mouthful. "That's just Ginny. Pretty hot though, huh, Mom?"

"That's not an appropriate way to talk about a young lady," says

Karen.

I have to say somethin' to keep this goin', so I chime in. "Marcie says Ginny has got the major league hots for you, Jake, and besides, they say she's done about half the high school boys already."

"Did *what*?" asks Stephie, suddenly entering a conversation not meant for her hearing. Jake starts to laugh, but the Perfect Lady says, "You three shush up now. That's no way to talk at dinner. Jake, perhaps we need to have a talk after Henry comes home."

"Oh, Mom," he says. "Don't overreact. I can't stand having another one of those special talks about birds and bees and stuff."

"Besides," I say, "you don't have to worry — Jake's a fag." Jake kicks me under the table and laughs. "Yeah, right!" he says sarcastically.

"Like you're completely gay, man!" I continue.

"Enough," Karen says. "Do not *ever* use the word fag or faggot, and don't ever say gay if you mean it as an insult."

"Come on, Mom," Jake says. "Everybody calls everybody else gay or fag. It's just a joke. Hank doesn't mean anything bad by it. He's just kidding with me. There's no harm in that."

"Is it funny to tell jokes with the word 'nigger' in them?" she asks. "Is it funny to call Chinese people 'gooks,' or to call Jews 'kikes'? No, it is *not*. So don't use words that demean gays. It's just bigotry, and you should know better."

"That kind of surprises me," says Jake, who's the only one I know who can keep this kinda conversation going without making Karen lose her temper.

"Why?" she asks.

"Because Catholics say being homosexual is sinful, and so do a lot of people. You hear those fundamentalists talking about it all the time. They say that there's stuff in the Bible against it, that 'Jesus is against it.' You're real religious and you're real conservative. I'm just surprised you'd get upset when we kid about someone being a pervert even though we don't really mean anything by it."

"OK, honey," she says, using her patient voice, "let me explain something to you. First of all, Jesus said not one single thing against homosexuals in any of the gospels. But he does give us guidance. He says we should love each other, even the least amongst us, even our enemies, even people who we don't think are very loveable. Jesus is clear on that, and he says it over and over again.

"Now, the Old Testament, particularly *Leviticus*, includes rules calling homosexuality an abomination. Some people argue that the entire Bible is either literally true or the precise Word of God. So, they say, Jesus *must* be against homosexuality. But if they eat shellfish, or eat pork, or sell a daughter into slavery, or fail to heed dozens of other laws set down in the Old Testament, they're being hypocrites because all those laws are in the Bible, too. And it is just not possible to know which laws God really means, and which ones he doesn't.

"But we can look at the central message that Jesus brought, and that was a message of love. There was no room for hate, and there was no room for mean-spirited name-calling. Regardless of what a person concludes about homosexuality, gays deserve the same rights and same respect and same dignity as the rest of us do. The fundamentalists seem to like to exclude rather than include. Their little God-club is pretty small, and nobody can get in except people who think exactly the way they do. They often are narrow-minded and mean-spirited people who see the world in black and white. The world, Jake, is gray, all kinds of shades of gray, and the only thing we have to hold onto is the unqualified love offered us by Jesus. I know that sounds sappy to you, but it's what I believe, and it's why you shouldn't ever speak in nasty ways about any other person."

It is vintage Perfect Lady — she gets so into what she's saying, her eyes almost glaze over, and she gets pink splotches on her cheeks. She seems a little like those TV evangelist types, who she says she doesn't like.

I don't think much about fags — it's just not something that comes up unless you're giving somebody a little shit. Kids my age aren't all hung up on that sex stuff. People can pretty much do what they want and we figure it's none of our business, at least the kids I know. We see enough weirdness not to get too freaked out over stuff that's a little off the wall.

I admit, though, this sex stuff is strange — real strange. If some guy gets as stupid over another guy as I get over girls, then I figure he's working with something that's pretty nearly bigger than he is. The only hope would be to go some place where people wouldn't make you feel stupid, and to do that probably means becoming like a hermit or something.

"Mom," says Jake, "don't get goin' on the God Squad stuff, OK? Hank and I just kid around and don't mean anything by it, and we don't hate fags… I mean gays. In fact, we don't give that stuff much thought at all."

The Perfect Lady refuses to leave it there — to let Jake have the last word. "Just remember, even jokes *can* hurt people, and you might not even be aware who you're hurting. Besides, acting like a bigot makes you sound stupid. It reflects poorly on you, and I don't want that, either."

The Perfect Lady gets up and starts to clear the table. "But I think we still have to have another talk when Henry gets home," she says.

Christ, do I ever hope I can miss that discussion. I think I'll try to slip away on my bike before it gets started.

Chapter 13

Unfortunately, my great escape attempt fails, and the after-dinner sex talk goes on forever. Even Dad falls asleep twice, twice getting the "Honey, are you listening?" question, followed by a sour stare and a few seconds of angry silence. The Perfect Lady says only one thing I hadn't heard before — that kids are getting VD from oral sex. But the last thing Jake and me are going to tell her is that she says anything worth hearing. I sit there, slouched down in the armchair, and Jake lays on his back on the rug with his feet up on the couch.

I spend some of the time trying to picture the Perfect Lady doing it with Dad, but I give up — it's too weird a picture. Stephie and Jake can only be the result of immaculate conception, I decide. That the Perfect Lady would get naked and hump around in the sack just doesn't seem possible to me. But I sure can picture Dad — in fact, the picture won't go away, though I sure wish it would. I have trouble even looking him in the eye these days, and when he makes one of those rare attempts to talk with me or do something with me, I usually just clam up and say I'm busy. I don't like knowing the stuff I know about him. It's changed the way I see him, and not for the better.

A few days earlier, after dinner, Dad gets a case of the guilts and makes one of those dufus attempts to be my buddy. "Want to throw a ball around?" he asks.

His question catches me by surprise and, I say, "sure," before even thinking.

So out to the backyard we go. He throws hard and straight — probably was good before he got to be old. He tries to bring up stuff he thinks I'll find interesting, but we've got nothin' in common. I talk about the O's and baseball because that stuff is safe.

I say that I'm real pissed off by this guy playin' for San Diego. According to the papers, he's got two wives — one, in Mexico, is pretty poor and has a bunch of kids, and the second is a real hot babe, who's some kind of soft porn star, who he keeps in a fancy condo in La Jolla. Around his neck, on a chain, the guy wears this WWJD (What Would Jesus Do?) gold charm, and points at the sky every time he hits a home run, which is pretty often. I wonder if he actually believes God cares who wins a stupid baseball game. I wonder if he thinks God loves him more than the poor slob of a pitcher who he's just clobbered. I wonder a lot of stuff like that, but I just say to Dad that the guy's a real A-hole.

Dad seems to be listening. "Who knows what's going on with him, Hank?" he says. "Who knows why he does what he does? People are weak. People make mistakes. It's hard to really understand him unless you walk in his shoes."

Yeah, right! His little talk is almost as annoying as Karen's. I know too much. No way I should listen to him on this subject.

Anyway, after Karen finishes her sex-ed lecture, we head upstairs to Jake's room, and before I even get the door closed, Jake says, "So, tell me what Marcie says about Ginny."

I tell him everything, including the party coming up this Saturday night. He surprises me by saying he wants to go, and I ask him how he's gonna pull that off with the jail-keeper/watchdog-woman running the show. He says he'll sneak out after everybody's asleep. That's not too rough, actually, since the Perfect Lady collapses around ten.

I say that I'm not gonna risk getting caught 'cause of the thin ice I'm on in that house already. I'll go over to Sue's, I say, and tell her exactly what I'm doin' Saturday night. She'll be cool with it and won't even press me for details. On Saturday night, she and Pete'll be stoned, watching some video, and eating their pizza. I'll be able to stay with them, no hassle, and then go to the party.

Jake and I agree that, if I can get Marcie and Ginny to pick us up at the Hereford WaWa, we'll meet there. I know Marcie's got to get her sister to cooperate, but when I call, that turns out to be no problem. Marcie's sister says the time is good since she and her boyfriend will be done watching some movie down at Hunt Valley and will be heading to the party about then anyway.

It works perfect. Come Saturday night, Sue and Pete, as usual, pay no attention to me. And Jake tells me that, just as I predicted, the Perfect Lady crashes right at ten. Jake just climbs out his window, hangs from the sill, and drops onto the ground. I'm waiting at the WaWa when he cycles up, and we stash his bike behind the store with mine. This is the first time we've gone to a party with the older kids and we're pretty psyched up about it. I'm not showing it, but I'm a little nervous about it, too.

As usual, I'm not really sure how to act around Marcie. I don't even know her all that well except from classes and lunch and stuff. I guess she pretty much has got this scene figured out and knows what she's doing. As for Jake, I can't really tell what he's thinking — except he's got Ginny on the brain. Her rep has got him believing he's gonna be "Stud of the Week," but that would just about scare me shitless. I mean, I like the idea and stuff, but I don't have a clue. That's why, last spring, I had pretty much decided to avoid all this girl stuff until it stopped making me feel retarded, assuming it ever stops making me "King of Geek Central."

But here I am at WaWa with Jake all confident that he's gonna do something exciting with Ginny, and me wondering why in the hell Marcie wants me to go to a party with her. But as freaked out as I am, I also feel this rush about what's going to happen. In the pit of my stomach, I kinda feel that this is way cool 'cause it makes me feel older. It makes me feel free — like I'm doing shit without anybody telling me what to do or how to act. I think I like that, even if it does make me nervous.

George, who is Tina's boyfriend, comes hauling into the WaWa lot in a big green Suburban van at about 10:35 and we pile into the back two seats — Jake all the way in back with Ginny, and me in front of them with Marcie. Marcie and Ginny have on their halter-tops and cutoffs, they're wearing lipstick and eyeliner and stuff, and they smell good.

George is wearing a St. John's lacrosse T-shirt and holding a beer. He turns out to be an 11th grader and has that cocky private school look you see on those kinds of kids. It's as though he always knows the score before the game is played and as though absolutely nothing is a big deal to him. He's real casual, the kind of kid who wears sunglasses when there's no sun. He and Tina don't even look in the back or say anything when we get in.

We drive on Mt. Carmel over to York Road, go right on York, and then left on Monkton Road until we hit Blue Mountain. Then I sort of lose track. Marcie has hold of my hand. I can hear Ginny talking to Jake real quiet, and Marcie starts telling me how lousy her boss was the last few days and how much she's been looking forward to this party. And on and on she goes, which is perfect because I can just sit there hearing her voice, smelling her perfume, feeling her hand in mine, and feeling her pressing against me. I think I could probably just sit like that, near an open car window with the summer air blowing in on me, pretty near forever.

We take a left into a driveway and I can see we're driving into some kind of horse farm. Cars are parked on pretty narrow patches of grass on both sides of the driveway. About three hundred yards in, George spots an empty patch just big enough for the Suburban, swings it through, and stops, turning off the car.

"OK boys and girls," says George, turning around to look at us for the first time. "Be back at this car no later than one. If I'm not here, sit and wait for me, 'cause I'm leaving at one or whenever I feel like it after one and I don't want to waste my time looking for you. Got it?"

Jake says loud and sarcastic, "Yes, sir! Whatever you say, sir!" Ginny giggles.

George exhales real hard and shakes his head, "Just be here, asshole, or you're on your own for a ride back."

We all get out. I'm holding hands with Marcie and Jake is doing the same with Ginny. We all start up the driveway, each couple separate from the others. We can hear the music, and we can see there must be a couple hundred people inside the lighted windows of this great big house.

Things get louder and louder as we approach. Tina and George go around the back. The front door is wide open and Marcie leads me through it. I look back and see Jake and Ginny standing and talking.

Inside is just unbelievable. There are kids everywhere. You have to push to get anywhere. There's no furniture at all that I can see and, in what shoulda been a living room, everybody's dancing like crazy people. The floor is wet and I kick a beer can as Marcie drags me through the crowd. The sliding glass doors are open and we go out back.

There are kids everywhere here, too. Some are in the pool, and all around it is this real nice furniture that looks like it should have been in the living room. We walk around the pool. Kids are making out. One girl has her halter-top off and she's slow dancing, with her breasts up against this guy in a bathing suit. They both have cigarettes and beers. I notice that most of the kids in the pool are buck-naked. I can't believe it.

Marcie keeps dragging me around until we go back through some other open doors into what looks like a dining room, but one table-leg there is broken, and, because of that, all these beer cans have slid off the table and onto the floor. The chairs must be outside. We push through into the kitchen, where the refrigerator doors are open and there are beer cans all over the floor. The cupboard, counter, and sink are all full of empty liquor bottles.

Stairs lead into a basement, and down we go. There's only one light on so it's hard to see much, but music's thumping, and kids are up dancing on this pool table. Everyone's drinking beer except this group in the corner we pass. They've gotten a whole bunch of wine bottles out of this humongous cabinet that has a shattered glass door. Some are opening bottles with a corkscrew. Others are swigging wine straight out of the bottles. I've never seen so much wine in one place except at a liquor store.

We push back through the room, me trailing behind Marcie like some kind of puppy on a leash. I can't believe the stuff I'm seeing. Back up the stairs we go, back through the living room, through the front hallway, and back out the front door. Out front, it's a little quieter than inside or out back.

Marcie turns and looks at me and I can't think of anything to say except, "Wow!" so I say it and feel like a nerd, but she says "Wow" right back at me. She lets go of my hand and sits down on the grass, so I sit next to her.

"I've never been to a party like this," she says.

"Me neither," I say. We sit there for a few minutes.

"Whose house is it?" I ask.

"Some guy named Mark Dunbar. He's in the eleventh grade at Baltimore Grammar. His folks went to California, and left him alone in the house. At least that's what Tina told me. Did you see anybody you know, 'cause like I didn't see a single person *I* know?"

"They're all older than us," I say. "What's gonna happen when his parents get home?"

Marcie shakes her head back and forth. "I don't wanna be around when that goes down."

"Me neither," I say. "It's a big house and it's pretty much trashed."

"You wanna look around some more?" Marcie asks me.

"Sure," I say, "but what more is there?"

"Upstairs," she says. "We can check out upstairs."

We have to shove our way through bodies to get up the stairs. At the top, there's a bathroom with the light on, and a guy on his knees, hugging the toilet. I look in and another guy is asleep in the bathtub. He's holding onto a wine bottle, and it looks like he's puked all over himself. The sink is completely full of puke and there's even puke on the floor. It's too loud to talk, so Marcie makes a real "gross-me-out face" and pulls me back out into the hallway.

There's a closed door down on the right, and Marcie opens it, but hits some guy who's standing in the way and taking pictures. He sorta moves to the side, and we squeeze in. On both sides of a bed are all these guys making faces. They're all watching a guy who's on top of a dark-haired girl. She's got her legs wrapped around him and she's smiling at the camera over his shoulder. He's humpin' away like there's no tomorrow.

He stops and gets off her and she starts posing and stuff. Then another guy pulls off his pants and lays down on the bed with her. Then another guy gets naked and climbs on the bed… and then another! Now there're three guys and this one girl, all wriggling around on the bed. All four of 'em are doing stuff and this guy is snappin' away with the camera. One guy who's watching shakes up a beer bottle and starts squirting beer all over the kids on the bed, and then everybody starts squirting beer.

I'm just staring. I can't believe it, and then I realize that Marcie's pulling on me, real frantic to get out of there. Except for the girl on the bed with the three guys, Marcie's the only girl in the room, and this scene is totally uncool. I can see why she's freaking out, but I'm just staring like a zombie.

She manages to get the door open a crack and we squeeze out. She's half running down the hall, pulling me behind her. We stumble down the stairs and out onto the front lawn. She's breathing really hard, and when she turns, I can see she's crying. "I gotta find Tina," she sobs. "I gotta go home."

We start around the side of the house and walk toward the pool. At the shallow end, I see about six couples having chicken fights in the water. The girls on the guys' shoulders all have their tops off. There's a crowd standing around them, cheering and clapping.

Just as we get to the other side of the pool, four guys come up behind a real nice couch where a couple is making out, and they pick it up and toss it all — including the boy and girl — into the deep end of the pool. People start screaming and shouting and all of a sudden all the furniture is being tossed into the pool. Marcie doesn't see Tina, so she drags me back around to the front of the house. "Let's go to George's car," she says. "Maybe they're back already."

"OK," I say, "but it's only about eleven-thirty." Sure enough, nobody's there, but Marcie wants to stay, so we climb into the back seat. She's still crying quietly, so I put my arm around her and she leans her head on my shoulder. We just sit there that way for a long time until she sits up and says she needs a tissue.

She crawls up over the front-seat center console and finds what must be Tina's purse underneath the front passenger seat. She pulls out a little package and throws the cloth purse back onto the front seat. She blows her nose and wipes her face. Then she leans forward and looks in the rear view mirror. "I'm a mess," she says.

And then she sits back down and puts her head back on my shoulder. My arm's around her, and it's quiet except for the music coming from the house. It's pretty dark, and she still smells good. This sure beats the shit out of that party.

My mind is jumbled up with snapshots of the stuff Marcie and I just saw — beer on the floor, the broken leg on the dining room table, the furniture in the pool, the naked chicken fights, the kids with all that wine in front of the broken cabinet, the puke in the bathroom, the girl with those three guys on the bed with her, the guy taking pictures, and the guys spraying beer on everybody and laughing. It goes round and round in my head too fast to make sense of it all.

Then Marcie says in a soft, little-girl voice that reminds me of Stephie, "Why would those boys want to do that to her? Why would she let them?" She kind of shudders against me, and I hold her a little tighter, but can't think of much to say, even with all those pictures flashing through my head.

So I just say, "I don't know." After a moment or two goes by, I think of a little more to add, "It makes me kind of sick, I think" — real deep stuff, I know, and I'm thinking how dumb I am when she tilts her head back to look up at me.

"Me too," she says. "I felt kind of sick and sad and confused."

"Yeah, like that," I say, looking down at her. She reaches her hand across, puts it behind my head, and sorta gently pulls my head down toward her. Then she kisses me real, real softly on the lips. I kiss back, and we do that for a long time, and I'm thinking I could do this for just about the rest of my life.

But then she stops and sits up and looks at me. "I hope Tina is OK," she says. "I hope she's OK with all that stuff going on."

"We'll go find her if she's not here by one," I say. "Jake and Ginny will be back by then, and they can help us."

"OK," she says, and presses up against me. I turn toward her, and she reaches around me and gives me a hug. We kiss again. She runs her hands up under my t-shirt and starts rubbing my back, which I like a lot. Then, while we're kissing, she sticks her tongue in my mouth. I like that even better.

She's definitely in charge of this stuff, and I'm kinda scared to do much on my own. I can hear Karen's voice in my head — "treat girls with respect," and "always ask before you do something." It just about drives me around the bend that anything Karen says is wandering around in my brain, especially at a time like this, but it is.

Marcie seems to get stuff a minute before I figure it out. She pulls back and runs her hands around under my t-shirt and over my chest while she's looking right at my face. She then takes me by the wrists and puts my hands on the sides of her rib cage and slides them under this tight halter-top she's wearing, and then she puts her arms around my neck and starts kissing me again.

Now, I'm not sure, but this strikes me as a pretty clear signal that I might be able to put my hands on her breasts without having to ask. So, soon I'm rubbing them and stuff, and when her top rides up, she starts pushing me backwards. Before I really get what's going on, I'm lying backwards on the seat and she's half lying on top of me. She sort of pushes off me, our hips touching and her hands on my shoulders, so I can see her breasts above me. She lowers them toward my face and I just kind of kiss 'em and stuff, not really knowing what's expected.

After a while, she sits up and pulls her top down. I'm thinking, "How does somebody our age have all this stuff figured out?" She just seems to know how to act even when she's with this clueless dimwit. Then she says, sorta outta the blue, "I'm a virgin you know."

"Oh," I say.

"Have you done stuff like this with a girl before?" she asks.

"No," I say, telling the truth only because lying would be too obvious.

"Well," she says, "I let a guy feel me up once before. That was in the spring, but that's it for me so far."

"Oh," I say again.

"All my girlfriends are doing all kinds of stuff," Marcie says. "You know, oral sex and stuff, and they talk about it all the time. It kinda scares me, though, and I know I don't want to have real sex yet. That's way too heavy."

"Oh," I again say, exhibiting my usual conversational brilliance.

"But if you really wanted to, Hank, maybe sometime I would let you touch me, and, you know, I could touch you." Marcie puts her head back on my shoulder and sort of snuggles up against me again. I get my arm around her and we sit there together with a little breeze coming through the window. I like her smell. I like her feel. I could just stay this way — her up against me — for a long, long time. This is good stuff, I decide. That's when Jake suddenly opens the Suburban door. Damn! I nod to him, without saying a word.

"Hey guys," he says. "What's goin' on?" Ginny is there behind him.

"We're waiting," I say. "Did you see that party? Can you believe that stuff?"

He starts climbing in the car. Ginny gets in, too. They squeeze way into the back. "We didn't get though the front door," says Jake. "We just hung out in the front. It was quieter and not so crowded."

"And romantic too," Ginny says, and I can see she's all snuggled up against him. Now Jake winks at *me*.

"Geez, Jake," I tell him, "they've trashed the whole house. There's furniture in the pool, and people upstairs doing group sex stuff, and naked chicken fights…" It was as if all those snapshots were again tumbling from my brain and into my mouth.

"Slow down, partner," says Jake, leaning forward and placing his hand gently on my shoulder. "Slow down so I can understand you."

"They're trashing the house, man," but before I can say more, we feel a crash against the driver-side front door. I see Tina, and she's bending over George, who's now lying on the ground. His legs are sticking straight out and he's leaning back against the bottom of the car door, sorta slumped over and laughing hysterically. We all pile out of the car and Ginny does her super "I-don't-miss-a-thing" act by say-ing, "He's drunk."

"No shit, Sherlock," Jake says.

"How're we gonna get home?" I ask.

"I'm fine, man. I'm perfectly fine, and I'm gonna drive this sumbitch and you little assholes right outta here." George is talking like his tongue is about five sizes too big for his mouth, and it's hard to understand him.

"I'll drive," Tina says.

"No you won't," George slurs as he struggles to his feet. "This is my goddamn car, and I'll drive it. I'll drive it 'cause I have the frig-gin' keys, and 'cause I can, and 'cause I'm Richard Friggin' Petty. So if you wanna get home, get in. If you don't, screw every last one of you and the pig you rode in on. That's funny," he screeches, and then he starts to laugh hysterically again. He staggers around a bit, then falls down again, holding his belly and laughing this crazy, high-pitched gig-gle.

We all just sit there looking at him. He finally staggers to his feet and starts toward the car. Tina stands in his way, but he staggers right into her. "You're not driving," she says.

"The hell I'm not," he says. "Now get out of my way!"

"Let him try," Jake says to Tina. "He'll never get his sorry ass out of this spot without tearing up the car."

I look at the situation and can see Jake is right. George's super-sized Suburban is tightly wedged, one car on each side of his. In front of him is a post-and-rail fence, like the kind you'd see on a ranch. And beyond the fence are a bunch of trees.

"Knock yourself out," Tina says, and she steps aside.

George manages to get into the car, but we all watch from a

safe distance. First, he can't find the keys until he figures out they're in his pocket. Then he can't get them into the ignition. When he does get the car started, he puts it in gear, real deliberate like, and then twists around to look backwards real, real, slow. But then he hits the accelerator much too hard and goes flying *forward* — straight into and through the fence — all the time looking backward.

All of us chase the car out into the field, but it takes George about 25 feet more to get the thing stopped. The Suburban is now stuck up to the axle in soft dirt, and one of the fence rails has snapped off, piercing the van's grill and radiator. The rail itself is wedged into the ground. No matter what we try, we can't budge the Suburban, much less pull it out.

George is just sitting in the car, blubbering about how, if his father finds out, he'll be grounded, including an upcoming vacation in Bermuda. "What am I gonna do?" he asks no one in particular.

What a pathetic creep! I think.

That's when it dawns on me that we're also in hot water. I catch Jake's eye and can see that the same thought has occurred to him, too. I say to Marcie, "How're we gonna get outta here?"

"I dunno," she says. "*Our* parents are out of town."

Tina, who's listening, says, "Whatever you do, I gotta stay with George. He's a mess."

Things don't look good at all. Marcie and Ginny talk. Tina tries to comfort George, who's just sitting in the driver's seat, crying, with his head on the steering wheel. Jake and I try to figure out what to do, but we don't even know where we are. Marcie comes over and says she and Ginny are gonna stay with Tina until George sobers up. Then they'll find a way home with Tina.

That's not an option for Jake. George won't be sober for a long time, and Jake's gotta get home and into the house before the Perfect Lady gets up. Besides, things are just too weird in that big house up the driveway. The stuff those kids are doing there is over the edge, it scares us, and we don't want to be associated with it.

That's when Jake, in that stubborn voice he sometimes uses, says something that scares me and at the same time makes me realize I won't be able to change his mind. He says simply, "I'm calling Mom."

"No way, man," I say. "She'll go completely nuts. God knows what she'll do to us."

He shakes his head. "We're in trouble," he says. "We got to get out of here, and we can't wait. If it's as bad as you say, Hank, then it's better I get in trouble with Mom than hang around here with a house being torn apart and some kind of weird sex going on. Somebody's gonna get hurt."

The rest is history.

Jake goes into the house and sees for himself what's going on. He finds a phone and somehow gets a-hold of the Perfect Lady. He comes back and tells me we have to wait for her on the front step. He's pale, and on our walk back, he says that the kids in the house are now dragging everything out and throwing it in the pool. The refrigerator got pushed over and it landed on a guy. Jake watched it happen while he was on the phone. The guy's leg was a bloody mess, and he was screaming like a banshee.

The Perfect Lady arrives about twenty minutes later, her car creeping up the driveway right to the front door. We get in. She says nothing, doesn't even look at us, as we start out. "Mom," says Jake, who's next to her in the front, "there are some girls who need help," and he tells her where they are. She stops right by the spot where George went through the fence.

Jake gets out and gets Tina, Marcie, and Ginny to come over to our car. Karen says to them, "Get in," and there's something about her voice that makes it impossible for them to say "no," so in they get.

Karen asks the girls where they live. They tell her, and all the way to Ginny's house, Karen doesn't say another word. Ginny starts to get out when Karen asks, "What is your father's name?" Ginny tells her. Karen writes it down. "Your phone number?" Ginny tells her. Karen writes the information down. We pull out, and it's silence all the way to Marcie and Tina's. As Marcie and Tina get out, same questions, and Karen writes it all down. Karen drives me to Sue's house. I get out. She pulls away.

Not one word to me, either.

Chapter 14

Sometime Sunday morning, Jake tells the Perfect Lady the whole party story, and she immediately grounds him for the rest of the summer. Until school starts, she says, all he can do is work around the property and read. That also means no more baseball for Jake this summer, playoffs or no playoffs.

It turns out that, after we left with Karen, some kid at the party called 911, to get help for the kid with the broken leg. After the ambulance came, some cops arrived, and when they did, the kids threw beer cans at them, and then ran off. More cops came, made a bunch of arrests, and impounded all the cars — that cost everybody a bunch of money and caused them some major problems getting home.

The party even made the *Baltimore Sun*, and all the kids eighteen or older got their names in the paper. Now, there's some party news in the *Sun* almost every day. The Dunbars say they're going to sue for the damage the kids did to their property — about $100,000 worth. A bunch of parents say they're suing the Dunbars for not supervising the party the right way. Everybody is blaming everybody else for what happened.

That includes Marcie. She and Tina say that Karen, who took names and numbers, ratted them out to their parents. And they say that, because of what Jake and me told Karen about the party, Karen called the cops and got everybody in trouble. Actually, it wasn't Karen, and it wasn't us — the 911 people did it, I'm pretty sure. But everybody believes it was us, so it doesn't matter what the truth is. What matters to me is what Karen says — I'm not welcome at her house until she says so. Marcie won't talk to me. I can't see either Jake or Stephie. I have to stay at home with Sue and Pete, who go to work every day. I can either watch TV or go out on my bike during the day. At night, I watch more TV with Sue and Pete or just screw around on the computer.

Sue's cool with the whole party thing. I didn't have to lie much to her about it, and I didn't sneak out or anything to get to it, so she didn't punish me at all. But the whole thing sucks. No Jake. No Stephie. No Marcie. No friends in the whole county. No nothing.

I don't mind doing things by myself — I've always got the Gunpowder and my bike. What bothers me most is knowing that I can't do things with somebody else even if I want to. Most of all, I miss seeing Stephie and Jake. I miss them lots. Sue and Pete don't pay any attention to me, which doesn't bother me, except I'd like to be able to talk to someone who actually listens and who actually cares what I say. Talking to Sue is like talking to myself. She kinda fades in and out on me. She's always saying things like, "What'd you say, honey?"

One day after the party, I take a long bike ride — all the way up the Gunpowder Trail from York Road to Pretty Boy Reservoir. It's one of those ninety-degree steamers where you sweat standing still. Not a single fisherman is on the river, 'cause it's a Wednesday. I pedal past the dried-up frog pond but don't feel like looking at it. I go past the place where we put the dead carp in the water, but it long ago rotted off the line and floated away.

I go in for a swim. It's like ice on my skin, so I don't stay in long. The path goes higher on the ridge and the sun's just right, so I look down and see trout — big lazy-looking trout just finning in the pools. The water flows past them, but they barely move. I see a king-fisher fly low over the water, and a great blue heron standing com-pletely still on the twigs from a beaver dam. The beavers have been working at night. The newly downed trees still have fresh looking yel-low stumps. The dam is larger than it was just two weeks ago, and the river above it is wider by almost a hundred yards.

The river seems to change every time I look at it, which, in a way, really annoys me. I can't even count on the Gunpowder to stay steady in its banks. On a map, I guess the Gunpowder looks the same as it always does, but on the ground, it's always different. The guy who makes decisions about water levels makes some of that change. Every day, he seems to release different amounts of water from the reservoir. The rest, as far as I can tell, is due to some random shit.

While I'm riding up the trail to get onto Little Falls Road, I'm thinking about Top and Fred. At least on Saturdays, I can mess around with those guys. They're about all the fun I got left this rotten summer. I also wanna go to that August paintball jamboree up in Pennsylvania that Top mentioned. It sounds way cool, camping outside and cooking food on a fire and playing war games with a whole bunch of other peo-ple. That would sound like good stuff anytime, but at this point in my bummer of a summer, it might keep me from going completely crazy with boredom.

I ride past Jake's house and stop at the driveway. I watch for a while, but there's no action. Everybody must be inside. I can hear the central air working away. Karen's car is in the garage, but Dad's is gone.

I wonder how much of a fight Dad put up when Karen told him I couldn't come over until "further notice." He was the one who called me up and gave me the bad news. He said I'd "made my bed," and now I "had to sleep in it." He promised that he and I would still get together at least once a week. It's been two weeks now and I haven't heard diddly from him. He must be "working" real hard, with emphasis on "hard," if you know what I mean. I don't expect to hear a thing from him.

It's about six o'clock and the mosquitoes are starting to get active. The gnats are swarming around me from the sweat. I've got about a half hour ride ahead of me, so I push off. For some reason, I feel like crying. I have a burning feeling in my throat and my chest feels tight. I ride like a maniac, pedaling like I'm in a sprint race, and pretty soon I'm out of breath. I get to the top of a steep hill, and go shooting down the other side, not braking at all, and I cut the curves into the wrong lane like I'm on a Kamikaze mission.

But no cars come around the bends, so now I ride with no hands, screaming at the top of my lungs like I'm charging an enemy machine-gun nest. They're shooting and shooting, but they miss me and they miss me some more. I'm dodging bullets, totally fearless, totally awesome, totally out of control, and all by myself. Nobody sees me do the battle. Nobody sees me fight the fight.

When I get home, I'm breathing heavy, but the tightness in my chest is gone. I'm just tired — real, real tired. I leave the bike in the garage and go in. Sue and Pete are — *what else?* — drinking beer and watching TV. It's around seven, so I plop down to watch the news with them. I say, "Heh!" They say, "Heh" back. I get a Coke and bring each of them another beer. They say thanks. There's Chinese in the fridge, I notice, so after awhile I throw rice and some kinda noodle veggie stuff into the microwave. The food gets hot in a coupla minutes. I eat leaning against the kitchen counter — the whole thing in just a few big bites. Then I throw the bowl in the sink.

I go down the hall to my room and pull off my clothes, leaving them on the floor beside all my other dirty clothes from last week. I go into the bathroom and turn the shower on. It gets hot and I step in. It feels good on me and I just stand there for a long time with my mind completely blank. Then I think about the party and all the stuff going on there — all that broken furniture and the puke and the guys and the girl. That picture-show just keeps running around in my head.

Then, for some weird reason, I think of Mr. Finks. If somebody told him about the party, I don't think he'd believe it. I can hear him saying in his distracted way, "You must be mistaken. I'm sure it couldn't happen the way you say." He would quote something from a famous poem, and maybe talk about the "better angels of our nature" or something just as weird.

I think of his little baby doing battle with the devil, and of the communion wafers falling like snow in our church. I think of him crying in class over that Ben Jonson poem. I'm starting to feel sad again.

I think of Cal Ripken's bad back, how he misses most of the season after playing every game practically forever before then. He's old and people say he ought to retire. He can't retire, but I know he will. He's been the man for the O's my whole life, it seems. I can't even think of the O's without him. Some things aren't supposed to change. But at the end of this season, I know he *will* be gone.

My mind just runs across all this stuff, and then I think of Marcie and the car, and I wonder what it would be like if I was able to see her again. The water is beating down on me. Thinking of Marcie makes me stiffen up, so I start to choke my chicken real slow. It takes awhile, and the water's lukewarm and then cool before I finish. It's not like any other feeling — this giant release. It's like an emptying, and all the time I'm thinking of Marcie. But then it's over, and I'm alone in the cool water, and I feel even worse than when I got in. I get out, dry off, go to my room, and pull on some clean shorts.

Out to the living room I go. The O's are on the tube tonight. I grab another Coke and plop down on the rug to watch. It's the bottom of the second, and the Yankees are already up by three runs. The O's great old leadoff man and centerfielder, Brady Anderson, is at bat. The Yanks' pitcher makes him look silly. Three pitches. Three strikes. He's out and back to the dugout in about thirty seconds.

Chapter 15

The paintball road trip is a go. Pete and Sue say they just want to take a few days off in Ocean City, but I can tell they want to go alone. That's pissed me off all summer, but now it fits my plan. "How come I never get to go to Ocean City?" I ask Sue. "This summer really sucks!"

To my surprise, she says, "We'll take you with us this weekend, honey, if you really want to spend time with us."

"I don't," I say. "I just want to have some fun for a change. Maybe I'll ask Dad if I can stay over there while you're gone. Maybe the Perfect Lady doesn't have her panties in such a twist any more."

Sue doubts that, I can tell, but I say, "That's OK, right? If Dad says so?"

She says, "Yeah," and I can tell she's relieved to have me out of her hair. So I wait a day, and while Sue and Pete are watching the tube and drinking beer, I tell them: "I'll be going over to Dad's Friday afternoon, and I'll come back here after you get back from OC."

Sue's eyes never leave "Who Wants to be a Millionaire?" or Regis Philbin, who's saying something dorky. "That's fine, baby," Sue says, pretty absent-mindedly.

I'm home free! I suppose I ought to feel guilty about it, except Sue's probably happy. She and Pete are off the hook. They can have their fun all weekend, smoking their dope and lying on the beach, and not have to worry about me. And I'll be running around in the woods, finally having some fun of my own. What's to feel guilty about when everybody gets what they want?

On Friday, I ride to the WaWa and wait until Top comes crunching into the lot. Fred jumps out, and like a fat old yellow lab jumping around in excitement, he's real happy to see me. "You ready, Hank? You ready? Oh boy, this'll be good. Believe me, this'll be good!"

Top interrupts, "Don't pee your pants there, Freddy boy. We got some time before the games get underway, and I don't want you all worn out before we even show up."

In we go to the WaWa, and out we come. Top's got his coffee, I've got nothing, and who knows what old Fat Fred has managed to liberate from the evil WaWa? We find out in the truck.

"Watcha got, boy?" Top asks.

Fred, showing all his lousy teeth in that goofy grin of his, reaches up under his big old baggy t-shirt and produces one of those silver serve-yourself coffee things — you know, the kind where you pump the black button on the top and the coffee comes out. How he managed to hide it so completely is something I don't think I really want to know. Maybe it was up in his armpit. I don't drink coffee, so it doesn't matter to me, but I am curious.

"You like coffee, Top!" Fred says joyfully. "So I got you a whole bunch of it."

"Jesus Christ Almighty," Top says — real drawn out — "you sorry excuse for a human being! We better get the hell out of here before they notice that thing is gone!" We peel out of the parking lot onto Mt. Carmel Road before turning onto 83 North.

That Fat Fred *is* a magician. The coffee pot is huge and he got it out of that WaWa without a problem. When he got into the truck, I didn't see it anywhere on him and I was lookin' right at him. Being a good thief, I suddenly decide, requires real talent and skill, and Fred's got what it takes. He's calm and cool and slick as hell. Plus shoplifting takes a certain amount of courage, considering what happens if you get caught.

Fred's generous, too, because he likes to steal stuff he can give or share with other people. You got to admire the guy in a weird sort of way. Who's he hurting? Some big corporation? Who cares about them? If you think about it, Fred's a fat version of Robin Hood. He's a klepto, but still, he's really pretty harmless.

Then again, it's kinda sad that he can't help himself.

We ride in silence for a while until Fred says in a little kid voice, "Don't you like the coffee, Top?"

Top looks over at him and then looks straight ahead. "Thanks, Fred," he says. "But you gotta watch yourself. One of these days, you're gonna get caught."

I think I hear Top's voice in a way that's new to me. It's almost gentle. He seems to be trying to be nice to Fred, and Fred hears it, 'cause he starts to squirm around happily in the front seat. "Let's sing some Army songs," he says. "I wanna be an Airborne Ranger, I wanna live a life of danger, I wanna kill some Viet Cong."

Fred's yellin' out the words, and we start to shout and sing out all the cadences Top has taught us. The wind is whipping in from the windows and we're charging up the highway at about 90 miles per hour hollering like crazy people. Nobody can hear us but us, and it's just about as purely fun as anything I can think of. There's no one to tell us what to do or how to do it, and we're just screamin' for no good reason but because we feel like it. My lousy summer seems a long way away.

We go through York, Pennsylvania, but after we turn off 83 and the roads start to get small, I lose track of where we are. We're going west. That much I can tell 'cause we're headed toward the sun, which makes Top put the visor down in the windshield so he doesn't get blinded. The drive takes us up and down hills, and past fields that are high with corn or thick with wheat. It smells sticky and wet and hot like summer.

When we pass a bunch of black and white cows, I smell manure, and then cut grass. By one farm, I smell turned-over dirt, though I don't see why. We pass a tractor and I take in that fuel/grease smell.

There's no rain in the air. It's August humid, but when none of those late-day thunderstorms are around. The truck just hums along into the sun with the wind blowing on me just right, and I sleep some.

I wake up as we pull into a field, bouncing along in the ruts where the grass has been knocked down by trucks that arrived ahead of us. Pickups are parked all over the field. I see Confederate flag decals on lots of back windows. One bumper sticker says, "I own guns and I vote." We pull into a spot next to an old, olive-colored, beat-up sedan. "Look at that baby," Top says. "It's a 1971 Plymouth Duster. It's probably still got that great old slant-six engine under the hood. Those things last forever."

We get out and carefully examine the Duster. Its bumpers are rusted and there are dents and paint patch spots all over it. The left front fender is gray — it must've been replaced. The interior is black vinyl, and it's got a three-on-the-floor gearshift. There's a Confederate flag decal on one side of the cracked rear window and a Marine Corps emblem on the other. The rear bumper sticker says "Semper Fi."

"That baby would be a classic if they'd kept it up," Top says.

"OK, men. I gotta get us registered. You hang out here while I go do a little recon."

Off he goes, and Fred and me have nothing to do but stand there and wait.

Chapter 16

We don't wait in the middle of that field for long, though. I gotta pee, and Fred does too. Because we don't see any of those porta-potties anywhere, the two of us head up a little hill, toward a patch of trees about two hundred yards away. We walk slowly 'cause Fred gets out of breath real easy. When we reach our destination, Fred proposes a contest.

"OK, Hank," he says, "you wanna go for furthest or longest, 'cause it's hard to do both?"

"Let's do both," I say, and I'm real confident 'cause I'm about to burst.

"Good. Good. Good," Fred sputters. "Let's stand here and try to arc it right over that log there." He points at a log about eight feet away, and, with his toe, draws a line in the leaves, which he says we have to stand behind. So we stand side by side and pull out our monsters. "On your mark, get set, GO!" Fred says real loud.

And, man, do I ever put it past that log. I send it about eye high, right over the top, and don't even get the log wet. Meantime, Fred's not doin' so well. He gives the log an initial squirt, but then sends his stream about two feet short. "I win distance!" I shout, but I feel my ammo getting low, and after a few more seconds I'm on this side of the log and fading fast.

Pretty soon I'm behind Fred, then I'm just squirtin' a coupla last times, and finally I'm done. But Fred's showin' no signs of slacking off. He's making a puddle only about a foot or so in front of him, but the sheer volume is just awesome. He keeps going and going and he's grinning really proud.

As he finishes off with a few last squirts, he declares, "I am the King of Piss."

"You," I say, "are the King of Klepto, the Prince of Piss, the Duke of Dork, and the Fred of Fat." We both laugh.

Then Fred spots a broken-down old barn on the backside of the trees. There's a farmhouse, too, and it looks abandoned. "Let's check it out," I say, so we walk through the little woods, across a few yards of field, and up to the buildings.

The house is broken-down fieldstone that looks like it must have been white-washed once. The roof looks like rusted-out tin, and there're splotches of green where it still has paint. Some of the green shutters are still up, but they're all crooked and hanging at odd angles. There's glass on a few panes, but most of the window frames on the ground floor are pushed in. And there's no front door.

We look in, but the floorboards are rotten looking, and we don't want to fall through, so we just go around the other side. I trip as I go to look in one of the windows, and as I try to catch my balance, my foot catches again, and I fall to my knees. I land on something hard and flat that makes a hollow "bong" sound when I hit it. I feel around on the grass and weeds and vines — it's something metal. I feel around some more and discover a metal handle of some kind. I step off the hard thing and give the handle a yank. I get it to open about three quarters of the way. Fred looks down under it and says, "Root cellar. I seen one once at a place where we was doin' a sewer pipe job."

"What's it for?" I ask.

"It's where they kept stuff cool when there were no refrigerators," he says. "They hauled ice in chunks and put it down there in the cellar."

"I'm gonna go down and see," I say.

Fred says, "OK!"

The steps are stone. I go first and Fred follows. It's so dark that our eyes are pretty useless at first. We can't quite stand straight up, either, but there's enough room for the two of us to turn and look around as our eyes adjust to the dark. What we see are mostly broken down shelves, and broken jars, most without tops. It's cool and nice down there, though. We feel all alone, hidden from the world — secret.

We climb out, and Fred gives the cellar door, which is hidden away under all the weeds and vines, a kick. It slams shut, and it's hidden again — as if we never saw it. I think I'd like to have a cool place like this, back in a field behind some woods. It'd be mine, and I'd share it with Jake and Stephie, and the Perfect Lady could stay the hell away — Dad, Sue, and Pete, too, for that matter.

Fred and me now head over to check out the barn. Fred is looking at me, and I can tell he wants to say something, so I say, "What?"

"Can I tell you some stuff, Hank?"

"Sure," I say.

"This is real private stuff, but we're friends, right? We're paintball teammates. We have fun together, right?"

"Yeah, Fred, sure. What's going on?"

"It's a secret, Hank. Can you keep a secret?"

"Sure, Fred, sure." I'm getting a little irritated.

"OK then," Fred says, and he stops walking and takes a deep

breath. "There shouldn't be secrets between friends, and we're friends, and I trust you, and I don't have very many friends."

And then, after pausing for about three full seconds, he says simply, "I'm queer."

We both stand there in silence for what must be a lot of seconds. I think Fred must be holding his breath again. I gotta say something. "So what?" I say.

Fred breathes again.

"How do you know?" I ask.

"I just do," he says. "I've been a fag for as long as I can remember."

"Why do you call yourself that?"

"Why not?"

"Isn't that like 'nigger' or 'bitch' or 'kike' or some other kind of insult?"

"I never really thought about it 'cause nobody knows except Top, and he's a fag, too."

"*What*?" I say, more than a little surprised. "No! Really?"

"Yup, we've been together for almost ten years now. We take care of each other, and we keep the secret, and everything is good. He's the first family I got since my mom and dad threw me out for being a homo."

"That's the real reason?"

"Yup, that's the *real* reason. I knew I was different from the time I was about nine, but didn't figure out *how* different until I was about thirteen. Mom caught me kissing my best friend and told Dad. When I told Dad I liked boys and wasn't sorry I did, he threw me out of the house."

"Your parents just cut you off like *that*?"

"Yup, they didn't want a 'goddamn pervert living in their house.'"

"That's cold, man."

"Yup. And I had some real cold nights after they threw me out. The street is a real bad place for a kid to grow up. I wouldn't want that again. I was very sad, and very lonely."

"Have you seen your parents since then?"

"Yup, from a distance. I used to go up there to Bel Air and stand across the street from the Giant where Mom buys her groceries. I'd see her go in for her Friday shopping, and then see her come out with a cart."

"Didn't you ever try to talk to her?"

"Yup, one time. It didn't work out so good. I said, 'Hi Mom, it's Freddy.' She turned and looked at me. '*My* Freddy is dead,' she said to me. Then she got in her car and drove off. Not even a smile. That hurt me all over again, so I never did it again."

"That's awful."

"Yup. But things are good now. Top and me — we got a good life. We do our stuff. I got work. We have some money. We have some fun. We don't need much. I've never been so happy, and now I have my friend, Hank, who knows my secret."

We turn away from the barn and head back toward the parking field without saying anything more. We walk all the way to the woods before the silence breaks.

"Don't tell Top," Fred blurts out.

"I bet he already knows," I say, joking, but Fred doesn't get the joke.

"No, I mean, don't let him know that *you* know he's gay. It embarrasses him. He says he isn't 'one of them,' whatever that means."

"Why?"

"He was in the Army for twenty years, you know, and he had these 'urges,' as he calls 'em, but he couldn't admit it to anybody, not even to himself. He doesn't like fags, never has, and then he sort of figured out he was one. He's still not happy about it — says the whole deal disgusts him. I think he's all screwed up about it."

"And you're *not*?"

"Nope. It only bothers me if it bothers other people. I don't got the problems Top's got."

"OK," I say, "I'll be quiet about it."

We walk out of the woods and down the hill toward the cars and trucks. I hear Perfect-Lady Karen's voice ringing in my ears. I hate that I remember her homosexuality lecture.

I like Fred. Top is OK, too. I like the paintball games we play. I like riding in their truck. I'm not sure what sex has to do with any of that. As for me, I know I like girls, but I can't explain why. I didn't *decide* to like them. It just happened.

By now, Top is waiting for us alongside the truck. He's pacing back and forth, and he's looking really ticked off.

Chapter 17

When Fred and me finally get to the truck, Top demands to know where the hell we've been.

"We found an old farm house," Fred gushes. "That was after we had a pissing contest. We tied."

Top just grunts. He'd got us registered, he tells us, and says we'll be sharing a campsite with our new teammates. A paintball team needs eight players, and these other guys only had five, so we fit with them perfect.

We grab our stuff out of the truck bed and start carrying it down to a place near the stream, which is on the edge of the field away from the woods and the old house Fred and me discovered. We walk past lots of guys setting up their tents — big ones and small ones. Some people are staying in campers back at the parking field.

We finally get to the area with a stake and a sign that says "47." This is the spot for our tents. We have two of 'em, one for Top and Fred, and a pair of old Army canvas shelter halves for me. Top and Fred's tent, you can stand up in. It has a little awning at the entrance and is made out of light green nylon. They hang a Coleman gas lantern from a rope in the middle from the top. Overall, it's real nice.

Right next to us are these big brown canvas tents. They have a heavy, old look, like they've been rolled up in the back of a truck or in a garage or a basement for a long time. They smell moldy when you got close. Nobody's in 'em yet.

When we get all set up and store away our sleeping stuff and paintball gear, Top says, "Grab that little cooking pack and that cooler. I got the rest. Let's go."

"Where we goin'?" Fred asks.

"Across that little footbridge — to where we can have a fire," says Top.

"Why don't we just set up here?" I ask.

"'cause they want the fires away from the tents. You don't wanna cook where you sleep. Varmints get into everything. They got a fire site across the way designated for each tent site. Let's go."

It's an easy walk. The footbridge is a solid, well-built wood thing, and we cross it. The stream is nice, with a steady flow over a stony bottom. There are pools and shallows and an undercut bank. I'll bet some trout live under there, too. A sign saying "1 to 50" points to the right, and another, for sites "51 to 100," to the left. Another sign saying "Paintball Courses" points straight ahead.

The sun is setting and the mosquitoes are getting active. We go right, towards the end, passing groups of men fixing up campsites. There's a ring of stones in the middle of each little clearing. Logs almost six-feet long and big enough to sit on are lying on two sides of most fire rings, and men are sitting on them, talking and smoking cigarettes. I'm carrying the cooler, and it's starting to get heavy. I put it down a coupla times and rest. Top and Fred wait for me. Fred's carrying a little pack. Top's got a big one.

"This is not real convenient," I say.

"Nope," Top says, "but the guy who owns this property can do anything he wants with it, I guess. You get this many men in one area, you gotta have rules, you gotta be orderly. You can't have people doin' whatever they want. You'll get people takin' a crap where others want to sleep, and then there'll be fights. And you can't have people stayin' up all night drinking beer and swapping lies and laughin' and gettin' loud right next to people who're tryin' to get some shut-eye. Unless you like having everybody pissed off, you gotta have rules. Rules are good."

Well, that was a whole lot more than I wanted or needed to hear, but that's Top for you. I never thought about rules as good — just as a pain in the butt. *Whatever*! All I know is I'm hauling that damn cooler a helluva long way because of some rule.

We finally get to a stake with the number 47 marked on it. There, a group of five guys are sittin' on logs around a real smoky fire. They're all dressed exactly alike — black t-shirts with white letters saying, "Live free or die," across the chest, and camo pants, bloused at the bottom the way Top wears his, and green canvas jungle boots like Top's. All five guys have big beards. Three have their hair pulled back in ponytails. One just has stubble on his head, and the other's a bald guy.

As we come into camp, the bald guy stands. The others just turn their heads and stare at us. "You the fellas from Baltimore who're joinin' us?" the bald guy asks as we stop in front of them.

"That's us," Top says. "You boys are from Wilkes Barre, am I right?"

"That's it," the baldy says. "I'm Bill, and this here's Joe," he says, pointing to a guy with a long black beard who nods. "This here's Kevin." He's the stubby-headed guy, and he doesn't even bother to look at us. He's got a buck knife out, and he's whittling away on a stick, shaving off big pieces of yellow wood. "Steve's his name," says Bill, who points to a guy with a scraggly blond beard and wearing a

CAT hat. Steve touches the brim and looks at us. "And that on the end of the log is Pete." Pete looks up and smiles at us with a mouthful of teeth even browner than Fred's.

"Nice to meet you, boys," Top says. "People call me Top, this here's Fred, and this here's Hank." Fred is smiling that big goofy, "I-wanna-be-your-friend" smile. I say, "Hi."

"Well, make yourselves at home," Bill says. "You can put your gear under that tree yonder," and he points to an oak a few yards back from the log benches.

We go over to the tree and arrange our stuff. I don't like something about these guys, though I can't really figure out what it is that bothers me. Bill's the leader. That's easy to see. He's about five-foot-eight, but with a big chest and hard arms that make his black t-shirt fit real tight. When he smiles at us, his eyes are kinda dead and blank-looking. I'd guess he's almost fifty years old or so, judging from that kind of leathery, wrinkled look that older people get on their skin when they've spent lots of time in the sun. A Marine Corps tattoo is visible on one bicep, and the words Semper Fi on the other. He looks like there's no fat on him anywhere.

When we come back to the fire, Top must see the tattoos, 'cause he says to Bill, "Yer a Jarhead, huh?"

With no expression, Bill says "yeah."

Kevin looks up from his knife and his stick, and with a real sour face says, "We *all* were in the Corps, and you better be a Marine if you're callin' us Jarheads."

Top laughs. "Nope, I'm an old G.I. grunt, served in Vietnam, two tours in country, with the 101st Airborne. Now I'm an old, retired, first sergeant. That's why they call me Top. No offense intended."

Kevin looks down at his stick and starts to carve again. He says nothing. The stubble on his head is grayish-silver. His beard is short gray stubble too — just a little longer than his head hair. He's got deep creases on his forehead and big black eyebrows. His forearms are huge and covered with thick dark hair. He's as skinny as Bill, and probably about the same height. I'd guess he's an old guy, too.

"You serve in 'Nam?" Top asks Bill.

"Some."

"And *you*?" asks Top, looking towards Kevin.

"Some," says Kevin.

"How 'bout the rest of you boys?" Top asks.

Pete's the first to respond. "Too young for that, but Joe here was in the Persian Gulf conflict."

"My men here are both cherries," Top says, "but I think they'll do OK. We're glad to be signin' on with you. Anything need to be done?"

"Wood," Bill says. "We need more wood for this fire."

"Hop to it, boys," says Top, turning to Fred and me. "Get us some good dry, burnin' wood — on the double."

Fred and I head out of the camp, away from the stream and into the woods. Top stays at the campfire. There's no wood close by, but when we get farther back in, there's plenty of stuff on the ground. It's brittle, dry, easy to break up. So, before long, we each have huge armfuls that we're taking back to the fire. We're not gone for more than twenty minutes, but when we get back, Top's already settled in, sitting on a log with the Wilkes Barre boys, and finishing a story.

"… so this private, after a quiet night, goes out to check this anti-personnel mine he'd laid into the ground for his squad's protection — you know, the kind that's wired to protect the perimeter around the camp. He gets right close to it 'cause he needs to roll up and collect the wire for use the next night when the thing goes off. Shit! They was scraping pieces of him off the trees. Those slimy damn gooks had crawled in there, somehow turned the mine around without gettin' blown to bits, or bein' heard, and rewired the sumbitch!"

Nobody says a word but Pete. "Ain't that something," he says, pretty matter-of-factly. The rest just sit there. Kevin's still carving away. When he sees us coming, Bill gets up and shows us where to stack the wood. "One more load should do it for tonight," he says, so Fred and me start to head back into the woods while Top winds himself up to tell another war story. "One night up near Khe San..." he begins. We don't hear the rest of the story.

By the time we get back with a ton more of wood, the fire is burning high. A covered aluminum pot and a blackened kettle sit on fire rocks, right up against the flames. Steve has set up a little portable table and has a two-burner Coleman stove on it. There're two pots on the burners, and Steve is pouring egg noodles into one and stirring them with a long-handled spoon. I go over for a closer look and see two plastic bags with brown stuff in the second pot.

"What's that?" I ask.

"That's beef stew gettin' good and hot," Steve says. "It'll go over the noodles."

"You the cook?"

"Yup."

"Always?"

"Yup."

"Why?"

Steve stops stirring and gives me a look. "You sure ask a lot of questions."

"Sorry," I say. Steve's blond ponytail hangs almost halfway

down his back and sticks out through the hole in the back of his hat. His eyes are real bright blue. His beard has grown in uneven, and has splotches and patches. He's tall — well over six feet — but skinny and stoop-shouldered.

"I was a cook in the Corps," Steve finally answers. "I like doin' it."

"Oh," I say and turn back toward the fire.

Top and Fred are rummaging through our stuff. In the cooler, Fred's found a pack of hot dogs, the buns, and some ketchup and mustard. Top's found some plastic bowls, mugs, and spoons. He puts them down on the cooler top along with the rest of the food stuff. "We gotta get some long wet sticks to cook the dogs on," he says.

It doesn't take long to find them. There're plenty of willows by the stream. We sharpen up one end of each stick and slide the dogs on. Top goes to stir some beans in the aluminum pot, but burns his fingers trying to get the lid open and pulls his hand away fast. Kevin's watching, and I see him just shake his head. Top gets the lid off, and gives the beans a stir. They're steaming and bubbling, so he pulls the pot away from the flames. "Let's roast the wieners, boys," Top says. So we do.

The Wilkes Barre boys are all lined up by Steve's table. Each has a bowl and a spoon. Steve gives them noodles and then slops on a bunch of stew over the top. Each man tears off a hunk of bread from a big crusty loaf that's lying next to the Coleman stove, then comes over to sit on the log by the fire.

There's a cooler by Steve's table that Pete dips into. He pulls out a six-pack of Old Milwaukee beer and walks past all the guys on the log. Each one pulls a can from the plastic holder. Then Steve comes over with his bowl and he, too, grabs an Old Milwaukee before plunking down on the log. Pete takes a beer for himself and puts the extra one, still hanging from the plastic, next to Bill.

My dog is done cookin'. I take it over to the cooler and put it on a bun. Top brings the beans over, and I scoop some into a bowl. I get a Coke by cracking the cooler open just enough so the stuff on top doesn't slide onto the ground. Then I go sit cross-legged on the ground near the logs.

"There's room here, boy," Joe says, and he points with his spoon at the empty log space next to him.

"Thanks," I say, "but the ground's good for now."

Fred gets his dog and beans and sorta collapses onto the ground next to me. Top sits down on the log next to Joe. I can barely see across the stream 'cause it's getting pretty dark, but I notice for the first time that, though we're almost straight across from our tents, only maybe 100 yards away, it takes forever to get there 'cause you have to walk downstream to the footbridge and back upstream on the other side. Somebody could have come up with a better system.

Everybody's quiet while eating. You can hear the plastic forks and spoons scraping on the bowls. I can hear fat Fred smackin' his lips and chewin' and sorta snortin'. He keeps his mouth open while he eats, and makes more noise than a dog in its bowl. He gets up for more beans and another dog. The Wilkes Barre boys sit there until Steve's done. Steve gets up and goes to the stove. Joe and Pete follow him. He gives them seconds and then gives himself more. All three come back to the logs and sit back down to eat some more.

Top, who's finished his dinner, asks the group a question. "How'd you boys get to know each other over there in Wilkes Barre?"

There's no answer for a second or two until Pete volunteers that they're all in the same club.

"What club is that?" Top asks.

Pete starts to answer, but Bill interrupts, "It's a combination outdoor club and social club. We were all servicemen, so we shared an interest. That led us to paintball, so here we are."

"How do you get to join the club?" asks Fred, who's always eager to be part of something.

There was another moment of silence, and then Kevin speaks. "You gotta be a Christian, white, heterosexual man, and you gotta be invited to join by another Christian, white, heterosexual man who's already a member."

Kevin goes back to his carving, but his words seem to hang in the air. To me, there's something unpleasant in the way it all sounds. And I wonder what Fred's thinking. What would it be like to be queer around guys like this? You'd keep your mouth shut for sure, but you'd probably be kinda edgy and uncomfortable, too.

Pete gets up, and simply announces, "KP." He starts collecting bowls and spoons from the Wilkes Barre boys. Joe, who's also standing up now, gets the pots off the stove and grabs a bag full of what must be cleaning stuff. The two of them head off toward the stream. Steve gets up and begins to clean off the stove. He folds it up and does the same with the table. He stores them with other stuff that's neatly arranged under a tree.

"Shouldn't we go clean up our stuff?" I say to Fred.

"Yup," he says, and we start collecting stuff and head toward the stream.

By the time Fred and me get back, Top is settled in with coffee from the black pot on the fire. On the faces of Bill, Kevin, and Steve, we can see the flickering, yellow-reddish glow of light from the fire. Those three guys are mostly looking down, Kevin's still carving, and —

what else? — Top's still talking. We can hear him as we get closer.

"… so that corporal just started getting crazier and crazier every time we had to go out on night patrol. We started having fire-fights pretty regular and the body count was high. That's when I noticed an ear tacked on a post by the boy's hut. The next day, there was two ears. About two weeks later, the crazy corporal came out for night patrol with a whole ear necklace, about nine of 'em strung on a wire and just hanging down over his chest. It was spooky, but, boy, he was one good man to have with you on patrol."

Kevin spits a long stream of tobacco juice into the fire. He must've been chewing since right after dinner, and he looks up at Top just as mean as you can imagine. "If that happened," he says, "that sorry son-of-a-bitch shoulda been made to eat every one of those god-damn ears."

Top doesn't seem to hear the tone in Kevin's voice, nor does he seem to know when to shut up. "Oh, it happened all right. I seen good boys go crazy in combat. How can you blame 'em? They didn't ask for the shit they're swimmin' in. They're scared and lonely and just generally pissed off. Hell, just look at that mess at My Lai. Some god-damn liberal politicians back home wanted to crucify those boys for 'committing an atrocity.' Those guys are sitting in their safe offices and their safe living rooms, passing judgment on how a man in combat should act. You gotta be there yourself, walking in their combat boots, to voice an opinion that counts…"

"Stop right there!" Bill interrupts. He's sitting on the log, bent at the waist, with his forearms on his thighs and his hands folded together. He turns his head to look at Top. "We shouldn't talk about this no more. I've been there, I've got an opinion, and it sure as hell ain't the same as yours. My Lai disgraced the Corps. Marines don't kill children. Marines don't rape women. Ever. There's honorable combat and there's chicken-shit excuses about battle stress. What went down in that little hamlet was disgusting. The rest of us were straight Marines, so don't give us this shit that everyone turns into an animal just 'cause he's tired and scared and pissed off. That's just bullshit, just plain bullshit."

Bill stands up just as Pete and Joe return from the river. "I'm goin' over to the tent," he says, making sure there'll be no more discussion of the subject. "Good night," he says, and then he walks off into the dark.

Nobody says a word. Kevin sticks his knife into the log and walks into the woods. I guess he's gonna take a leak. Joe pulls out a box of Swisher Sweet cigars and offers them around. Pete and Steve take one, as does Top — and they all light up and smoke in silence. Now Fred says *he's* headin' back to the tent. We'd been sittin' there for only about ten minutes, but Fred was already noddin' off, and twice he nearly fell off the log into the fire.

I stay. I love staring into a fire. There's just no feeling like it.

Kevin comes back. He pulls his knife out of the log and sits down. He starts to pick up off the ground the little carvings he's made. I can see he's made a bunch of chess pieces. They look like pawns. Kevin's looking around on the ground. "Damn," he says under his breath, "I coulda swore I made six of these buggers. Now there's only five."

I look across the fire real quick at Top and catch his eyes for an instant, before he looks down. Top knows where the sixth pawn is. So do I. Fred dislikes Kevin. A few minutes later, the tent Fred and Top are sharing across the stream is aglow from the lantern inside. Inside the tent's thin nylon, moving slowly and deliberately, is none other than the "King of Klepto," the "Prince of Piss," the "Duke of Dork," the "Fred of Fat."

I can't help worrying that somebody sitting right here at the fire with me may dislike Fred as much as Fred dislikes him.

Chapter 18

Whenever you camp out, it's not as quiet as you might think. There's lots of noise at night — lots of buzzing and chirping. Also, the mosquitoes are thick. I'm not sure either one's why, but for some reason, I don't sleep well that night, so I pull my head out of my little pup tent, lie on my back, and stare at the stars. There isn't but a little sliver of moon, so the stars — crowds and crowds of them — just stand out. If you think of how many stars you see, your head hurts and you feel smaller and smaller until you just feel like nothing. By about 2 a.m., I'm asleep again.

Top wakes me up at six. I feel too tired to get up, but I do. I grab my paintball gun and my goggles. I pull on my fatigue camouflage pants and my olive-drab colored t-shirt, and put a camo stick in my pants pocket. Fat Fred is stumbling around in a daze as we head to the footbridge and up the other side of the stream so we can boil some water and eat some oatmeal. When we get to the site, three of the Wilkes Barre boys are standing near Steve's stove table, which he's starting to fold up, and where they're drinking coffee. Joe and Pete are at the river cleaning stuff. Nobody says nothing, not even "Good morning."

At about quarter to seven, Bill says, "Let's go." We head down the trail, and turn right at the sign pointing to the paintball courses. It's about a ten-minute walk, and all the other men are leaving their campsites for the seven o'clock rules meeting. There must be over two hundred of us standing in this clearing, which turns out to be command central. Everybody's in some kind of uniform, and they're all ages — a few kids like me, but mostly old guys in their fifties or so. Some guys have helmets and fancy goggles. Some guys have padded camo vests. There are some real fancy, high-tech paintball guns, too.

A dried-up lookin' old man with a megaphone stands in the bed of a pick-up. "Listen up," he yells into the machine, and the place gets quiet.

"I'm Jim Otto, and this here's my farm. You boys have been doin' a good job followin' the rules. You'll be welcome here next year if you keep it up. But I heard some boy peed in the stream. Don't do that! When you wash up after dinner, put some water in a pot or bucket, away from the bank, and don't throw nothin' — no food, no soapy water, no nothin' — into the stream. OK? I hope that's clear. In a minute, I'll have the GO times up on all six courses. Each team will get at least five slots for at least four of the different courses. Each battle lasts no more than thirty minutes, shorter, of course, if a whole team gets killed quicker than that. The chart will have times, team names, and course numbers. There will be two officials on each course. What they say goes. You say one word of argument to an official, and you're disqualified. You say two words, and you and your team can just pack up and go home..."

The man goes on and on till I almost fall asleep standing up. When he finishes, the whole group starts to move in different directions. We have about a half hour to inspect our courses. Each one is about a half acre to an acre, and has different set-ups — different combinations of trenches and mounds and barrels and barbed wire. There's a different objective on each course, too. One team is attacking. The other is defending. You get points, and the officials keep score. It sounds real cool.

"Sounds" is the operative word. The whole day stinks in more ways than it's even possible to describe. We lose all five battles, and not one is even close. Fred gets himself eliminated in the first few moments of each game. Whether he's attacking or defending, he's like a paintball magnet. Top doesn't get eliminated, but he basically does nothing to help us win. He hunkers down in one place and never moves. I don't think he hits a single target the whole time.

The Wilkes Barre boys work real well as a team, but they pretty much ignore us, and I get in their way most of the time, which really pisses them off. I get eliminated about halfway through each game. So it usually winds up being the five Wilkes Barre guys against eight on the other team. We lose big time. Our teammates are really disgusted with me, Fred, and Top. Because of our overall poor performance, we're eligible for only a coupla consolation rounds the next day. The Wilkes Barre boys even talk about leaving early on account of us stinking out the joint. What a disappointment! I thought it was going to be a great weekend.

We go back to our tents around six. I bring a big pot of water from the stream and try to wash off the camouflage-paint from my face. I use the t-shirt I was wearing all day and hang it over the pup tent. It's still hot, and I'm still sweating a lot. I pull my sleeping bag from the tent and spread it out in the shadow the little tent casts. I just plop down with nothing on but my shorts and stare up at the big, blue, cloudless sky. I drift off to sleep.

When I wake up, Fred's standing over me. His face is still smeared with some camo-paint, but he got most of it off somehow. "Hey, Hank," he says, "you hungry? I'm hungry. You hungry?"

"Yup."

"Let's go eat. Top's there already. I can eat lots of hot dogs."

I get up from the bag and pull on a t-shirt and my sneakers. It's already getting dark, so I musta slept for almost two hours, I figure. Fred and me trudge across the field.

"Those are not nice men," Fred says sadly. "Not nice men at all."

"Well, we *are* pretty bad!" I say.

"That don't matter. They don't have to act so mean. I don't like any of 'em, specially Kevin. He told me I was a waste of space and a sorry excuse for a human being."

"Don't worry about it, Fred. They're just real competitive. They want to win. Don't take it personal. I'm like that in baseball 'cause I care about the results too much."

"But you don't yell at your teammates when they make mistakes, do you, Hank?"

"I guess not," I say.

We cross the footbridge and walk upstream. Top is already cooking a dog. He must've gathered the wood himself, 'cause there's plenty. The bean pot is near the flames. The mustard and stuff are on the cooler with the bowls and spoons. Steve is cooking. Kevin is carving. The other three Wilkes Barre boys are just quietly sitting on the logs. Top looks up and sees us. "Grab your stick, and cook yourself up one of these dogs, boys. Beans are ready, too."

I don't know why he's so cheerful. He must be completely clueless about what those Wilkes Barre boys think of him.

I get my stick and spear a hot dog. Fred does too. Steve motions with his spoon and the four of them get up to eat — Bill first, then Kevin, then Joe, and then Pete. It's a little routine they seem to have worked out. When they sit down, I can see they have rice with a kind of creamy yellow gravy on it with chunks of chicken and carrots and peas mixed in. Our hot dogs are fine, but these guys are a couple of steps above us in the food department. Pete offers beers around, and same as last night, Bill grabs two.

There's no sound around the fire except the crackle of the burning wood and the click of plastic spoons and forks against bowls. Nobody has much to say. After dinner, the same wash-up routine occurs. Joe and Pete and then Fred and me head to the stream. By the time we're done, it's pitch dark out. Clouds must've moved in 'cause there are no stars.

Around the campfire, everybody is completely silent. Fred and me sit on the log. Joe and Pete come back and sit down. Everybody's there except Kevin, and his knife is stickin' out of the log where he usually sits, almost daring anyone to sit in his place. I don't. Joe, looking at Bill, asks, "Where's Kev?"

"Takin' one of his walks."

Out come the Swisher Sweets. Top gets offered one and takes it. Fred and me do, too. Maybe it's like a peace pipe. I say to Bill, "Will you tell me about being a Marine in Vietnam?"

He looks over at me for a second or two without saying a word. Then he says with a sigh, "not much to tell, son. I was a sergeant back then and in country from '67 to '69. Combat is not something you really want to talk much about. It is what it is — a lot of young boys dying far away from home on the orders of old men for reasons they do not completely understand. It's something I could've done without."

"Tet, huh," says Top, piping in. "I was there during Tet, too. Saigon was a mess…"

"Stop!" says Bill, holding up his hand. "No more of your happy horseshit stories, OK? Just spare me."

There's silence again —maybe ten seconds of it — and then Top says real quiet, "OK."

We sit smoking our cigars. I'm feeling real dizzy and sorta sick to my stomach, so I hold my cigar and stare into the fire. I'm also feeling completely apart from my family, mainly 'cause I'm with a group of people who I can't even get a handle on. And I'm feeling way in over my head. Jake and Stephie seem far away, far away.

Fred gets up and starts shuffling around the fire, poking it with a stick. He's tripping over people's feet and saying, "Sorry, sorry." And then I see it happen. I actually see Fred "the King of Klepto" do his magician-like thing. Kevin's knife goes from the log, to Fred's hand, and then to Fred's pocket almost faster than the eye can see. I sorta freeze. My heart starts to beat like it's going to jump out of my chest.

"I'm gonna hit the sack," says Fred in his usual goofy way, and he starts to shuffle off into the dark.

"Me too," Top says. "Wait up, Freddy boy," and he gets up. "Night all. See you tomorrow. You comin', Hank?"

My mind is just going nuts. "No," I say. "I'll sit here at the fire for a while longer."

"Suit yourself," says Top, who follows Fred down the trail.

Fred wasn't thinkin' things through. Kevin knows exactly where he put that knife. What the hell am I supposed to do now? Should I chase down Fred and Top and get the knife back? That wouldn't change things unless I can do it in secret. And then, what if I get caught with Kevin's knife? Or do I say nothing and hope they won't blame the theft on me?

These thoughts go through my brain like a speeded-up movie, like when the sound track goes real fast and the words run together so you can't understand them. I'm almost paralyzed. I sit real still on the log with the burned-out Swisher Sweet in my fingers, and I stare into the fire like a zombie. I know what's gonna happen. I can just feel it, and it's not gonna be good.

About ten minutes go by. Everyone around the fire is quietly thinking his own thoughts. I see the tent across the stream light up, and I just shake my head. That's when Kevin shows up. He goes right to where his knife was stuck in the log and looks straight at where he left it. He then looks under one side of the log, then the other. He feels around on both sides of the log and at the end. I stop looking at him and just stare into the fire. But I can feel that he's just standing there now, looking at us and thinking things through.

"OK, assholes," he says real slow. "Who's got my knife?"

They all look at him, then at the log, then back at him.

"It was stickin' there just a coupla minutes ago," Bill says. "I don't know where it's at now."

We all get up and look around. "It's gone," Steve says.

We're all standin' around the log now, and Kevin looks straight at me. "You know where my knife is, boy?"

"No sir," I say.

"Well, I reckon I know where it's at," Kevin answers, and he turns and walks into the woods, heading toward the footbridge.

They all look at Bill. "Should I go with him?" Joe asks.

"I believe he'd've asked for your help if he wanted it. He'll take care of the matter." They all nod, and we sit down on the logs again.

Bill pokes the fire with a stick. Pete's turning his cigar round and round in his fingers, staring at the ash. Joe starts paring at his fingernails with the short blade of his Swiss Army knife. Steve, playin' with some tobacco in a pouch, flicks his Swisher Sweet into the fire and shoves a pile of brown tobacco shavings into his mouth. The tobacco hangs over his lips until he pushes it in with an index finger. He works it around until it's all in his right cheek. He looks like a chipmunk.

Nobody says nothin'. But I hear every sound like it's an explosion, and with every new noise I feel like I'm gonna jump out of my skin.

The fire pops, and I jump. To me, the crickets and tree-frogs suddenly sound like they're roaring out of the woods. The stream is now an ocean of waves over rocks, and a splash — maybe a water rat, maybe a fish — makes my heart pound harder, then harder still.

My mind leaps from one thing to another. Fred's got the knife. Fred hides the knife. Kevin opens the tent. Kevin sees the knife. There's an argument. There's shouting... but I hear nothing like that. I hear all the sounds confused together. Then I hear fast footsteps pounding up the path and getting closer to us. I freeze. My heart is in my throat.

Kevin comes running into the camp. He's out of breath and just about completely red in the face. He starts to talk, but nothing comes out. All of the Wilkes Barre boys stand up and look at him.

"F-F-F-F-Faggots!" he screams.

"What?"

"Faggots!"

"What're you talkin' about?"

"I go to the tent," Kevin finally says, "and it's all lighted up, so I can see right in, and they're ... they're..."

"Are you sure?"

"Hell, yes! You can't make no mistake about that."

They all kinda look at each other, and then Bill says quiet but hard, "Come with me, boys." And they all start down the path toward the footbridge.

This is bad. No, this is serious. These guys don't mess around.

So what do I do now? The Wilkes Barre boys have all headed towards Fred and Top, but they've forgotten about me. I look across the stream, toward the lighted-up tent, and I decide. I gotta warn Fred and Top and, if I take a slightly more direct route, I think I can get there before the Wilkes Barre boys! So I race down to the water and strip off my sneakers, shorts, and underwear, leaving them on the bank. I splash through the waist-high water, holding my t-shirt high, and scramble, bare-assed, up the bank and to the tent.

"Top, Fred," I whisper real loud. "Kevin knows you stole his knife. And he saw you two together in the tent. They're all coming to get you. Run away! Fast!"

Top and Fred fumble around for a few seconds, then dash out the tent door.

"Shit, what do we do?" Top says in this scared voice I hadn't heard before.

"Hide," I say. "Fred knows a place. Take him, Fred. Go and stay there. Go there now!"

They turn and run, disappearing into the night. I've never seen either Fred or Top move so fast before.

I turn and sprint back to the stream, splash back across, and pull my shorts and sneakers back on. I stand real close to the fire and rub my legs to dry off faster. I'm out of breath and I'm scared. I've helped the thief and I've helped the "perverts." I'm one of them, but I'm not *with* them. They're hiding! I'm staying. I'm different. Maybe. Maybe not.

I turn to look across at the tent, and the Wilkes Barre boys are just getting there. One of them unzips the front door. Someone says, "They're gone." I can see from the shadows that they're all standing there. Then they're gone, too.

I'm dry now. I sit on the log, and I wait. I can't run away. Where would I go? Maybe I should have gone with Top and Fred. But I'm not a thief. I'm not gay. I shouldn't be in trouble. I shouldn't need to hide.

I don't know what to do, so I do nothing. I just sit and wait. They'll be back, and I'll know nothing.

What'll happen to me then?

I don't have a clue.

Chapter 19

Waiting can be long and lonely, but the end of a long wait can be even worse. When all the Wilkes Barre boys finally show up together back at the campfire, Bill is in front.

"Hank… that's your name, isn't it son?"

"Yessir."

"Where are your friends?"

"I dunno. In their tent maybe?"

"Don't act stupid," Bill says — pretty snippy.

"Nossir."

"Are you a thief?"

"Nossir."

"Are you a homosexual?"

"Nossir."

"But your friends are."

"Nossir."

"Come on, son. Don't play dumb with us. Tell us where your friends are."

"I dunno, sir. I don't know what's going on." And then I start to cry. I'm not faking, either. It just happens. They all stand there, watching me blubber. Then they move a few yards away and have a discussion I can't hear.

Bill turns and walks back to me. "Come on, son. You'll stay in my tent tonight."

I get up and go with Bill. Kevin's right behind us. The others follow behind *him*. It's quiet all the way to the tents. Bill unzips one and says to Joe, "Stay with him." I go in. So does Joe. The others stay outside.

Bill tells them in a low voice — one that I can just barely hear — that Steve will keep an eye on the vehicles. "Make sure no one leaves," he instructs.

Pete will search Top's tent. Kevin and Bill will walk through all the tents from opposite directions. They'll all meet back at Fred and Top's tent in 30 minutes.

Joe and I sit in the dark of the tent. He says nothing. I say nothing. I wonder if Fred and Top have made it to the root cellar, as I had told 'em. I wonder if they're OK. I daydream about Stephie on her bike. Time, surprisingly, goes by fast.

When Pete returns from Fred and Top's tent, he announces that he's found Kevin's knife and the wood pawn. "Damn!" Kevin says. "I knew I'd carved six."

Pete has also found Top's truck keys. "They're goin' nowhere without these," I hear Pete say. "And here are their boots."

"OK, here's the plan." It's Bill's voice now. "We'll get some shut-eye. It's too dark to find anybody now. At first light, we'll search the whole area. We'll figure out which is their truck, and then we'll hit the roads if need be. Those two sad pukes can't get very far without their boots. They're probably just sittin' in the woods, hiding ... OK, let's turn in."

Bill and Kevin come into the tent I'm in. Kevin throws me my sleeping bag. "Go to sleep," he says. Kevin drags a cot over in front, and unfolds it so it's completely blocking the tent entrance, and lies down. Bill plops himself down on the other cot. I stretch out on the ground, just lying on top of my bag.

I don't think I can sleep, but it seems like about two seconds later when I feel this foot pushing me. "Wake up, boy." It's Kevin. "We're goin' for a walk."

As I come out of the tent, I see them all standing there in a group. Mist is coming off the stream. The grass is wet with dew. The day has that gray look that you see just before the sun breaks the horizon. There's no activity in any of the tents. The place is still — except for us.

Steve comes right up to me. "Where's their truck, boy?" he asks. They're all looking at me, and I don't want to tell them.

"Come on, son," Bill says, "we'll find it anyway." And I know he's right. There's no use pretending I don't know, and maybe they'll think I'm being cooperative if I tell them. I point across the field at the red pickup. "There," I say.

"Right next to our Duster," Steve says.

Bill starts layin' out plans. "Steve, you drive their truck around the local roads. Take Pete with you. If you see 'em, put 'em in the bed of the truck and bring 'em back here. Be back by noon."

Steve and Pete leave for the truck. Bill turns to Kevin. "Take Joe with you," he says, "and search the east side of the stream. Work by grid, south to north. I'll head up to that hill yonder," and he points to the trees where Fred and me had our pissing contest. "And I'll take the boy with me. Be back here by noon. Let's go, son," he says to me.

We walk toward those little woods. Bill stays slightly behind me but close enough to reach out and grab me. If I could run, where would I run *to*? And if I ran, wouldn't he catch me? I decide not to take any chances.

We come to the trees and we stop. Bill looks around. We can see to the stream and past it from our little height. We can even see down the road we came in on. Fields stretch out to our north a ways. Then there are woods. I notice when Bill spots the old barn and house. He bends over and peers through the trees, straightens up, and looks at me.

"Your friends are perverts and thieves, and we don't take kindly to either one. Go easy on yourself, son, and tell me where they are. They're not worth protecting. "

I say nothing.

"They gotta be close," says Bill. "No shoes, no truck, and they're both sad, outta-shape sacks of shit who'd rather sit than walk."

We stand quiet for a while. Bill bends over and stares through the trees again. "Stay close to me, son," he says, starting to walk again. We walk through every inch of those trees. Bill even looks up into the branches of the big ones. The thought of Fred climbing a tree strikes me as pretty funny, and I almost laugh out loud.

Then Bill walks into the field on the other side of the trees and stares down at the barn and the house. He points to the right, and we start down around the house, with Bill checking it out real careful from a distance. We walk past the buildings, across the field, and into another patch of trees some hundred yards past the buildings. This is a bigger wood than the others, but Bill's just as thorough.

The sun is getting higher. It's turning into a hazy, thick day. I'm sweatin' even in the shade. We come back out from the trees. Bill stands and stares at the house. We walk back towards it, but on the other side this time — with Bill stopping every few seconds to stare at the buildings. We don't go up to the house, and I'm not sure why right then, but Bill answers the question for me when we get back to the pissing woods. We walk in far enough so it'd be hard to see us, but where we have a good view of the house. "Sit down," he says to me, and I do. So does he, and he leans his back up against an oak and makes himself comfortable.

"It makes too much sense," he says. "They've got to be in that house yonder. They've probably seen us walk by twice now, and they'll think we're done looking. They'll be coming out presently, so we'll just sit here and watch for awhile."

He's right. It does make perfect sense. We wait and wait, and the sun gets higher, and the day gets hotter. Bill keeps looking at his watch. After what seems like forever, he gets up and says, "Let's go." We walk down the hill toward the tents. Everybody else is there. We're the last ones. "No luck," they say.

"I do believe they're holed up in a house and barn over yonder," Bill says. "Let's all head on up there."

Back up the hill we go, right past the pissing log, out the backside of the woods, down the hill, and right up to the house. I'm betting that Bill's right. In fact, I'm sure Fred and Top are in the root cellar, where it's cool, and where they're just waiting for night to come so they can escape. One thing those two can do is sit still, and they know all the paintball people gotta be off this guy's farm by 5 p.m. Sunday. I'm scared now. The two of them are down in that cellar, and Bill's gonna find them there.

What will they do with them then? I can't figure that one out. They've already gotten Kevin's knife back, *and* the missing pawn.

But that's not what's really got them hot. It's gotta be all the gay stuff. For some reason, it makes certain people crazy. I heard about that gay kid, somewhere out west, who got tied to a fence post, then was killed, just because he was gay. And I know the football jocks at school all talk a lot about killing "faggots." Whatever these Wilkes Barre guys are gonna do when they find Fred and Top, I figure it's probably just as bad.

The men fan out around the house. Kevin says he's going inside. Bill and I go around the back, where we're not too far from the root cellar doors. I know exactly where those doors are, and I figure somebody's likely to trip on 'em, just like I did, because they're practically invisible.

Then I get an idea. Nobody'll look where I'm sittin.' Nobody'll stumble over a spot I'm on top of. So I say to Bill, "I'm tired. I want to sit down. I'll be right here where you can see me, right in plain view."

Bill looks at me for a second. "Don't do anything foolish, son," he says, warning me against an escape. "Go ahead and sit, but stay right there."

I wander over to the root cellar door and sit down on it. Bill watches me. Then he continues his search. Fred and Top must be wetting their pants down there in the dark. They must've heard our voices. They must've heard me sit down. It's strange being so close and yet so far away. I'm in hot, bright sunlight. They're in complete, cool darkness. I see what's going on. They can only guess. But — and this is real weird — I don't even know for sure if they're underneath me. They might be gone already — might have gotten the hell away last night. I might be scared for no good reason, and helping them for no good reason, too.

I'll say this much for them — I may end up outfoxing them, but these Wilkes Barre boys *are* thorough and persistent. It's hotter than hell out here — I can feel I'm getting sun-burned — but they search for hours, looking in every corner of that farmhouse and barn.

Bill comes to about five feet away from where I'm sitting, puts his fingers in his mouth, and whistles. The group gathers right in front of me. The wind is picking up. Big clouds have started to rise in the sky.

"They ain't here," Kevin says.

"Nope," Bill says. "They ain't." There's a long pause. "That's it then," Bill continues. "Let's pack up and go home." He turns to me and says, "Come with me, kid."

I get up. Fred and Top have escaped! They've made it — and maybe with my help.

But do the Wilkes Barre boys think I've helped the "faggots"? I guess I'll soon find out.

I follow them up the hill, through the trees, and back to the tents. They start packing up, and I start to go to my tent. Kevin stops me. "Leave it, you little faggot. You just sit there." Steve, Pete, and Joe go across the stream to get the cooking stuff. People all around are packing up and leaving. I could make a run for it, but Kevin stands over me, and Bill is nearby, taking down the tents.

When the others come back, they help Bill knock down and pack up the tents. Then they carry all the gear over to a little Toyota pickup that's on the other side of the Duster from Top's truck. They load the stuff in the bed. Kevin never leaves my side.

Bill says to Joe, "You go back up and fix up their gear real nice. Got your knife on you?"

"Yup," Joe says, and off he goes.

Kevin says, "I'll take care of the engine." Bill moves over close to me.

Pete says, "Me too."

I see Kevin stick his knife five or six times into the rear tire of Fred and Top's pickup. Kevin kicks the side of the truck as he moves forward toward the front tire, and he scrapes his knife along the paint. He bends over, and I can't see what he's doing to the front tire. Pete's around on the other side. I hear banging. Then Kevin's in the cab. I can't see exactly what he's up to, but he's in there for a long time.

Pete yells, "Pop the hood," and the hood clicks up. Pete raises it, stands on the front bumper, and leans into the engine. Every few seconds or so, he pulls something out and tosses it onto the ground. When Joe gets back from the tent, they're done with the truck, and the truck has gotta be completely wasted!

We gather again behind the Toyota. "We're all set," Bill says. "Just throw those truck keys as far as you can, Steve." Steve follows orders. "Now let's take this little faggot and put him in the trunk." He points to me.

Kevin opens the Duster trunk and tells me to get in. I do. Joe comes and tells me to lie on my stomach with my hands behind me. He duct tapes my wrists together. Then he duct tapes my ankles together and rolls me over. He puts a piece of duct tape over my mouth. They close the trunk, and it's dark.

I'm way past being scared. I'm half-crazy with fear.

Chapter 20

Even before their Duster starts moving, I fight back tears, realizing that if my nose stuffs up from crying, I'll suffocate and die.

Then we bounce out of the field, which hurts. I'm lying on a car jack and across a spare tire in a cramped car trunk. The ride becomes much smoother and less painful when we get back on the road, and I try to lie still in the dark.

After some time goes by — hard to say how much — I start trying to figure how I might get myself out of this mess. I bend way over at the waist like a jack knife and realize my arms are almost long enough to squeeze my butt through them. This is the first time I've ever been happy about being a skinny kid with no butt. I wriggle and push. I sweat like crazy. My shorts start to slide off and, as they do, I push as hard as I can, and my hands make it under my butt and are free.

Now I go fetal, pulling my legs through. The first thing I do is pull the duct tape off my mouth. Boy, does that make a difference! It takes a while, but I manage to get the tape off my wrists, and then I free my ankles, too. Things aren't good, but they sure are better. I feel almost happy. Funny how that works. There I am, happy in the trunk of a car, going someplace, I don't know where, just hoping these guys don't kill me.

And, of course, that happiness leaves as fast as it comes. I realize I'm hungry, real, real hungry, since I haven't eaten since yesterday's hotdog dinner. I'm tired, too — the kind of tired that makes your arms and legs feel heavy. I figure the road must have gotten wet 'cause the regular hum of the tires now has an added hissing sound — water spinning off the treads, I guess. I feel myself drifting off to sleep, and I dream.

In my dream, Stephie is riding her bike round and round the house. I'm standing in the driveway, calling out her name, but for reasons I do not understand, she cannot hear me. Jake comes in the driveway on his bike and goes right by me like I'm invisible to him. I say, "Hey," but he can't hear me either. I yell out their names again and again, but they don't know I'm there. Stephie gets off her bike and skips up to Jake, who is now heading inside. She gives him a hug, and they walk to the kitchen door, holding hands, and go indoors.

I look through the kitchen window, and suddenly Perfect-Lady Karen is looking at me. She shakes her head back and forth, looking me right in the eyes. Real slow and deliberate, she pulls a cord and closes the blinds. I get on my bike and ride as fast as I can. After a little bit of pedaling, I pass Mr. Finks, who's walking down the road. I say, "Hi, Mr. Finks." He turns and looks at me. "Do I know you?" he asks, sounding real puzzled.

"It's *me*, Hank."

"I don't know any Hank," Mr. Finks says as he turns and starts walking away. I watch him until he disappears from view. Then I pedal real fast again and reach the Gunpowder.

The sawed-off guy with the baby in the backpack is there, but the backpack is empty. The man is fishing and crying.

"Where's your baby?" I yell at him. He looks at me with tears on his face, and he at least seems to hear me. He shrugs his shoulders and keeps fishing. I watch him and he catches nothing.

I ride real fast again down the Gunpowder path, and now *I'm* crying. I get to the frog pond, and it's full of frogs — little ones and big ones. I leap off my bike and into the shallow water. I start shoving frogs into my pockets, but they keep slipping away and falling out. I try to scoop them up in my arms, but I can't hold them. They're scared, but they don't want my help. "Run away," I yell to them. "They'll get you if you don't run away! Run away fast! Hide!"

I wake up — and it's no dream. The car has stopped. I hear the engine turning off. I feel the Wilkes Barre boys getting out, and I'm scared again! The doors slam. Then there's silence. They don't open the trunk. I hold real still, hold my breath, and listen. Nothing. Where did they go? I lie there, and then realize what's up 'cause I'm so hungry. They've gone in to get some food. They're probably at a restaurant or in a grocery store, and have left me alone in the car.

"Gotta get out," I practically scream at myself, but how? I feel the jack in my back and start to grope around for the tire iron. I find it. Then I feel all around the trunk with my hands and find the back of the seats — from the passenger part of the Duster. It's not all metal — it's softer to the feel, and it gives a little when I push. I start to hit it with the point of the tire iron, and the iron sinks in. I do that about 20 times, and I'm making a hole. Some light comes into the trunk, but not much. It must be dark out. I work the tire iron back and forth. I hit the seat hard, over and over. I'm sweating. I'm panting like a dog. I gotta work fast. They'll be back soon. I gotta get away — now!

The hole into the backseat is at last getting larger. I kick the edges with my feet. I pull and tear with my hands. I shove my head through the hole, and finally I can actually see the backseat. A dozen more hard kicks, a rip, and I squeeze through the hole. I push the passenger side seat forward, and open the door.

Now I'm out and running in the darkness and the rain. I don't look anywhere, I just run. I run down the road, then into the woods. I run and run until I can't run any more.

I lie down on my back and my chest feels like it will split open. I'm breathing so hard I can't get air. I'm choking, I think, and I can hear squeaking, breathing, and wheezing sounds. They're mine! I try to be still, and I begin to catch my breath. My chest feels better. But then I think, "They looked long and hard for Top and Fred. They took almost a whole day. They'll come for me, too."

I get up and start to run again — not a sprint this time, but a real steady jog. I dodge trees and push through vines. I'm going farther and farther into the woods. When I start to lose my breath, I walk fast until my breath gets better. Then I run again. For hours, I do this alternating jog/fast walk. I do it until I practically run into a high chain-link fence.

Through the fence, I see a big highway. Trucks and cars are going by fast. I climb the fence and walk along the other side of it. I walk until I feel I'm gonna collapse, but then I see an overpass. When I get to it, I walk up an exit ramp and look at the signs. The highway's marked "Pennsylvania Turnpike." There are signs pointing east and signs pointing west, but they don't help me any. I don't know where the Pennsylvania Turnpike is relative to Baltimore.

I walk to the edge of the road, back into the woods a little, and I sit down, out of sight of the cars. I'm soaking wet. My clothes are torn. I have scratches all over me. I can see that it's starting to get light out. It must be Monday morning by now.

Nobody in the world knows where I am — not a single person. And, as far as I can tell, no one cares. I think of Buck from *Call of the*

Wild. He was all alone. I think of Alaska and *Coming Into the Country*. That's where I need to go. I'll get on the highway, stick my thumb out, and head west.

I'm not thinking well. I'm too tired, too hungry. "Sleep, then find someone to give me some food," I say to myself, "then get on that highway going west." There's nothing for me back in Baltimore, I decide. Karen pulled the shade on one part of my life. Sue and Pete would rather have me out of their way. After that party, I've got no friends my age. Everyone thinks I ratted them out. Maybe I can get a fresh start somewhere else. I don't know how.

Nothing's clear. Everything's confused. I just want to slip away, become a trout in the Gunpowder — like a shadow, here and then gone, seen and unseen, and then maybe safe. As a trout, I could slip way back under a river bank, with food floating downstream to me, laughing at those guys in their silly rubber pants who wave their rods in the air, curse, and try to catch me.

But then, if the sawed-off guy comes by, I'd let him catch me. He'd show me to his baby, and she'd love my pretty colors and try to touch me, but he'd laugh and put me back in the water, real gentle, and I'd swim away, back to my hiding place, and maybe he'd catch me again another day.

Chapter 21

When I get up off the ground and stumble down the hill toward the turnpike, my legs feel like heavy stones. It's light out now. The shadows of trees are long and skinny. More cars fly by, and I wait for a coupla minutes to cross the two eastbound lanes.

I get to the grassy median. It hasn't been mowed, so hundreds of wild flowers — yellow and red, purple and pink — are growing out of control. I just stand there, numb and stupid, staring at the flowers with a blank brain. I try to look east, up the westbound lane where the cars come from, but the sun is right in my face, low and mean just over the highway. I can't see jack-shit, so I just turn like a cow, put my back to the glare, and stare west at the cars coming at me with their windshields shining bright from the sun.

All the drivers have their visors down. Most have on sunglasses. I watch their set, grim faces staring straight ahead till they're even with me, and then they turn their heads to look. For just a tiny second, they see me, and I see them, and then they're gone, vanished from my sight, continuing into that blinding sun.

There's a pause in the traffic, and in the distance I see a car moving slower than the others. It's almost out of its lane and onto the shoulder. I watch it as it comes toward me. It gets close, and I can see the front bumper's on at an angle. It's an old, beat-up station wagon. I can hear it kind of shimmying over the highway joints without the hum-thump smoothness of the faster cars. The driver has his visor *and* his side window down. He's got his arm hanging out of the car, kind of slapping the door as if in time to some music or something.

When he pulls abreast of me, his head turns like all the others, but he's got no sunglasses on, so our eyes lock. And holy shit if it ain't old Mr. Finks with those silly long strands of hair blowing around his bald head! As he goes by, he nearly breaks his neck staring over his shoulder at me, and I manage to make a little wave. His brake lights go on and he swerves real sudden onto the shoulder. He drives about one hundred yards past me, then starts backing up. I turn toward him, staring, but I can't move. I just stand there, locked in place.

When he gets even with me, he stops and gets out of his wagon. He waits for a few cars to pass before waddling across the two lanes like a fat hen chased by something. When he reaches me, he stops, out of breath, and pauses for just a split second.

"Hank? Is that *you*? Hank Collins? And what in heaven's name happened to you? Holy Hannah, you look a mess. Come with me right now. This isn't right, you being here all by yourself in this condition. "

And he steps toward me and puts his arm around my shoulders. I can't move. I stand there, but I start to shake. Sobs just come up from way inside me that I didn't know were gonna start, and I can't seem to stop. Mr. Finks grabs me in this big bear hug and we just stand there as the cars go by. My face is smooshed against his chest. He smells like soap, and pretty soon I stop crying. He lets me out of the hug, holds me by the hand, and leads me back across the eastbound lanes.

He takes me around to the passenger side, opens the front door, reaches in, and onto the backseat throws some books and papers and other crap that was piled onto the front seat. Then he steps back, motions for me to get in, slams the door after me, which rattles like it's gonna fall off, and comes around the front of the car to the driver's side. He gets in, slams his door, gets the motor started on the third try, and pulls slowly onto the highway after about a dozen cars go past.

We drive for about ten minutes, and he says nothing. The sun straight in my face makes it hard to keep my eyes open, and I fall asleep. I don't know how long I doze, but it can't be too long. When I reopen my eyes, Mr. Finks is stopping at some gas pump. I'm all sweaty, and the first thing I feel is a pain in my stomach like a cramp or something. I've never been so hungry, I decide. Mr. Finks looks over at me. "Hungry?" he asks.

"Yeah," I say.

"I'll fill up, and then we can go in for some breakfast."

"OK," I say.

We go into this place with restrooms and restaurants and Mr. Finks says, "Go wash up, Hank. I'll go into the Big Boy and order us some breakfast. What do you want? I'll order for you."

"I dunno."

"Orange juice?"

"Yup."

"Milk?"

"Yup."

"Pancakes?"

"Yup."

"Bacon and scrambled eggs?"

"Yup."

"The kitchen sink and the garden hose?"

"Yup... *What?*"

Mr. Finks smiles at me and pushes his glasses higher on his nose. "Go ahead and wash up, Hank, my omnivorous friend. I believe the operative word here is 'lots.'"

In the restroom mirror, I look like some sort of street person. I scrub the crud off my face and hands, but there's nothing I can do about the torn clothes. I go back out and find Mr. Finks sitting in a booth, reading a newspaper and sipping a cup of coffee. When he sees me, he folds up the paper and puts it down, then points to the seat opposite him. Big glasses of milk and OJ are already sitting there. I chug the milk down even as I slide into the booth, and I'm about to repeat the performance with the OJ when Mr. Finks says, "Whoa, Nelly Bell! Slow down there, Hank, or you'll spring a leak and we'll have to get the gas attendant to slap a tire patch over your navel."

"Sorry."

"No need to be sorry, son. I just don't want to see you chip a tooth raising that glass to your mouth."

The pancakes come. So do the eggs and bacon. I eat like I'm half-starved, which seems entirely appropriate given the circumstances. My whole self is into the food. Nothing but syrup and butter and pancakes and eggs and bacon and chewing and swallowing matters to me, and nothing else is in my head…Oh, I don't believe any food ever tasted any better than the breakfast in Big Boy that morning!

When I'm done, I push the plate away and notice there are still more glasses full of milk and OJ. I also see Mr. Finks watching me with a sort of sad, curious face.

"What?" I say.

"Have you had enough, Hank?"

"Yes, thank you."

There's silence. He takes a sip of coffee and watches me as I drink some more milk.

"Well," he begins, "I've had a good summer. My garden is healthy and my baby is crawling all over the house. I'm just back from a retreat in Ligonier, Pennsylvania. We did nothing but read and talk about Robert Frost…"

I interrupt. "Isn't that the thing you talked about in class — the thing that you do every summer?"

"Yes, yes it is."

"You and a bunch of teachers and professors talked about some guy who wrote about some wasted land."

"Yes, that guy was T.S. Eliot, and before him we did Joseph Conrad, and before him Charles Dickens, and before him C.S. Lewis. At my first retreat, we studied Emily Dickinson."

"I remember from class."

"I'm glad."

Then there's another long stretch of silence while I finish my OJ.

"We better push off," Mr. Finks says. "I promised my wife I'd be home by noon, and I believe we're cutting it a little close."

He pays the bill, which must be enormous, and I say thanks. As we walk out to the car, I get this heavy, sad feeling in my stomach and I don't think it's from the breakfast. I feel like I'm going to start crying again. But I don't want to, so I just turn my face toward my side window as Mr. Finks gets the car started, backs out, and starts toward the highway.

We drive for a while, and I'm feeling worse and worse. I don't want to go back to my life in Baltimore, but I don't want to go anywhere else either. My thoughts are coming fast. They're so jumbled that they make no sense. Just then Mr. Finks says, "Tell me, Hank, how has *your* summer been? Have you read any good books?"

"No," I say without turning to look at him.

We ride in silence for a while longer. "I seem to remember you were a pretty fair pitcher and shortstop," he says. "Did you play little league this summer?"

I don't mean for it to happen, but I turn to look at Mr. Finks just when he glances over at me. I see his eyes — those droopy, watery eyes that make him look a little like a hound dog. And just looking at him looking at me, all worried, with his hair blowing around his head... well... I lose it. I start to blubber again. It comes from deep inside me and I have no control over it. Mr. Finks pulls onto the shoulder and turns the engine off. He reaches over and grabs me and hugs and squeezes me so hard that breathing is now a major challenge. After a while, I stop crying, he lets me go, and we just sit there.

"Should we keep driving, Hank?" he finally asks.

I nod and he starts the car up again, and again we're back on the highway, doing about fifty in the far right lane. He looks over at me every so often, but he says nothing. That's when I start to talk, and I barely understand my own words, they come out so fast. It's like crying, almost out of control. It's like I'm puking up words, zillions of them. I don't even really know what I'm gonna say until I hear myself saying it.

I tell him stuff I never told anybody — stuff I didn't really even know I was feeling — and in an order that probably makes no sense to him. I tell him about Dad humping that woman in his office after the Orioles game.

I tell him about my big lie at school, about being a liar to him and even to Jake.

I tell him about quitting baseball because of all the practice-running.

I tell him about the big party, and how scared and confused I was there.

I tell him about Sue and Pete and their dope, about the Perfect Lady hating me, about purposely getting answers wrong on Crowley's tests and quizzes.

I tell him about kids hating me because they think I ratted them out after the party. I tell him how scared I am I won't get to see Jake and Stephie ever again.

I tell him how Sue didn't even notice my earring when I got it. I tell him how I wanted so badly to go to Ocean City with her this summer. I even called her "Mommy" by mistake, which probably would've embarrassed me if I hadn't been so quick to move on to the next thing.

I tell him how scared I am of girls and how I don't know how to act around them. I tell him about my battle against zits!

Then I tell him the whole story of Fred, Top, and the Wilkes Barre boys — of being trapped in the car trunk, of escaping, and of his rescue of me on the highway.

And then I sit there panting like a dog. I've run out of words. I've said it all. I look over at Mr. Finks. He looks over at me with that same hound-dog face, and then he looks forward.

"Hank," he says finally, "would you like to do some reading with me this summer — before school starts again? I've got some stories I'd like to try out on someone. I don't know whether they'll work for my seventh and eight grade students, and I need a thoughtful appraisal from a perceptive reader. You'd be doing me a favor. What do you think?"

"If you want," I say, looking at him, "I'll give it a try."

"That is fine," he says smiling at me. "That is *just* fine."

I stare out the window awhile and, from the barns we pass, realize we're on I-83. Then we cross my river and I wonder if anybody's down there — fishermen, tubers, paintball players, or kids on trail bikes.

"This Mount Carmel exit is where we get off for Sue's or Dad's house," I say to Mr. Finks.

"Where do you want to go?" he asks.

"I don't want to go anywhere," I say.

"Sue's is really home for you, isn't it?" Mr. Finks says.

"I don't have a home," I hear myself say.

He's quiet for a moment as he begins to pull off 83 onto the Mount Carmel exit. When we get to the stop sign, he stops and looks at me.

"Do you know what Robert Frost said 'home' is?" he asks.

"No, what?" I say.

"'Home is the place where, when you have to go there, they *have* to take you in.'"

"What's he mean by that?" I ask.

Mr. Finks takes off his glasses and rubs his eyes just like in class. "Well," he says, "it might mean different things to different people. But today, Hank, we're talking about you. What could it mean to *you*?"

"Well, I have to go someplace," I say.

"True."

"And I like eating better than not eating."

"I know that from recent observation."

"And I don't like being afraid in situations I don't understand."

"That's reasonable."

"But I don't like living at either Sue's or Karen's place."

"Does Frost say anything about what you *like*?"

I think for awhile. "No," I say. "It's where he says you *have* to go, not where you *want* to go."

"Right..."

"... and where they *have to* take you in."

"Right again," he says. "*Who* has to take you in, Hank?"

Again, I think for a while. "I guess Sue has to take me in 'cause she's got custody, and Dad should have to take me in 'cause he's my dad."

"So," says Mr. Finks, "you might have a choice then?"

"Yeah."

"What'll be your choice today, Hank — your choice right now?"

"I'll be better off going to Sue's," I tell him. "I'm not ready yet to answer anybody's questions, and Sue won't notice enough to ask me any, so let's go there — to Sue's."

"OK, how do I get there?"

I tell him, and we drive again in silence. We pull in the driveway, and there are no cars. It's Monday, and I'm guessing that Sue and Pete, back from the beach, are back at work already. My master plan has probably worked even better than I'd thought. Sue and Pete just think I'm over at the Perfect Lady's, and have gone off to work — business as usual.

I start to get out, but Mr. Finks stops me in my tracks. "Hold it," he says.

He begins to rummage around in all the crap he's thrown onto the backseat. He somehow finds a pen and some paper, and starts to write on a sheet, which he hands me. It has his name and home phone number on it.

"Your number, Hank?" he asks.

I give it to him, and he writes it down.

"I'll call you tomorrow, Hank, and we'll set up a schedule so that we meet at least twice a week — maybe more. Go to the library and get a copy of *Great Expectations* by Charles Dickens. We'll read some of that together."

"OK," I say.

"OK," he says.

I get out of the car and slam the door shut. He starts to pull away, but I still have my hand on the door, and I'm looking straight at him.

"Thanks, Mr. Finks," I say. "Thanks a lot."

Acknowledgements

More than anything else, aspiring first-time novelists need an opportunity to show the public their wares. For giving me the break that so many deserving writers never get, I am eternally grateful to Bruce Bortz, my publisher, editor, and friend. I also thank him for his wisdom and perceptive eye. Both have greatly benefited this work.

Without the nurturing support and encouragement of my family, I would not have survived the writing process, and so it is to them — Phyllis, Gregory, and Tyler Montgomery — that I dedicate *Hank*.

Kathy Imhoff, another friend and a former assistant, not only advised me on the contents of *Hank*, but also typed the first manuscript and then processed many of the subsequent changes for several of the next drafts. Absent her help and her sense of humor, I would have floundered.

Several first draft manuscript readers gave me useful advice and much-needed encouragement. Deserving of public thank-you's are Jamie Spragins, Meg Tipper, Richard Hawley, Jeff Christ, and Mark Trainer.

Thanks go also to President John Toll of Washington College, for so generously allowing me to work out of his marvelous liberal arts institution from a third floor office in the restored 18th century Custom House in Chestertown, Maryland. There is no more idyllic spot from which to think and write.

For providing a marvelous idea, wonderful inspiration, and a special night on Western Run, thanks to Tom Gamper.

In addition, I owe a real debt of gratitude to Joan Wang for her interest in and dedication to the successful promotion of Hank.

More generally, I want to thank my loving parents, both of whom are retired educators. My world-view was shaped by growing up with them on small school campuses, where students and teachers knew each other well. It was also shaped by four sisters who have generously tolerated my peculiarities lo these many years.

And finally, thanks to my many good friends, who have allowed me to fancy myself a writer without once giggling in my presence.

—Arch Montgomery

BALTIMORE ACTORS' THEATRE
CONSERVATORY